"I don't think I could shoot someone, Aaron."

"If it comes down to his life or yours or his and Sophia's, I think you could."

Tears filled her eyes, and she glanced up at him, not caring if he saw the wetness. "Yes, I could for Sophia." She sniffed, and a tear traced down her cheek. He lifted a hand and thumbed it away but left his palm cupping her cheek. She drew in a sharp breath.

"Clay will figure out what's going on. The man in the hospital will wake up eventually, and Clay will get him to talk."

Zoe closed her eyes against the lovely sensation of his touch. She had no business feeling an attraction for him. Not when she was fighting for hers and Sophia's lives. She opened her eyes and met his. "Aaron, I appreciate everything you and your family and friends have done for Sophia and me, but I think it's time for us to run again."

"How is that going to help?"

She sighed. "Well, for one, it'll give the authorities time to try to figure things out. But I can't run without help."

He frowned. "What do you mean?"

"I want you to help us disappear."

Lynette Eason is a bestselling, award-winning author who makes her home in South Carolina with her husband and two teenage children. She enjoys traveling, spending time with her family and teaching at various writing conferences around the country. She is a member of RWA (Romance Writers of America) and ACFW (American Christian Fiction Writers). Lynette can often be found online interacting with her readers. You can find her at facebook.com/lynette.eason and on Twitter, @lynetteeason.

Books by Lynette Eason

Love Inspired Suspense

Wrangler's Corner

The Lawman Returns
Rodeo Rescuer
Protecting Her Daughter

Capitol K-9 Unit

Trail of Evidence

Family Reunions

Hide and Seek
Christmas Cover-Up
Her Stolen Past

Rose Mountain Refuge

Agent Undercover
Holiday Hideout
Danger on the Mountain

Visit the Author Profile page at Harlequin.com for more titles.

PROTECTING HER DAUGHTER

LYNETTE EASON

HARLEQUIN® LOVE INSPIRED® SUSPENSE

Recycling programs for this product may not exist in your area.

TM LOVE INSPIRED BOOKS

ISBN-13: 978-0-373-67738-2

Protecting Her Daughter

Copyright © 2016 by Lynette Eason

www.Harlequin.com

Printed in U.S.A.

God is our refuge and strength,
A very present help in trouble.
—Psalms 46:1

This book is dedicated to those in law enforcement.
Thank you to the men and women who put their lives
on the line every day to make the world a safer place for me
and my loved ones. "May the Lord bless you and keep you,
may He make His face to shine upon you. Amen."

ONE

Zoe Collier gripped the pitchfork and stabbed it into the bale of hay. "I'm going to grab some water bottles from the fridge, okay?"

"Okay, Mom." Nine-year-old Sophia turned the water off and started wrapping the hose.

"Remind me to put some in the fridge out here for later."

"Put some out here for later," Sophia dutifully said.

"Haha. Come on in after you finish that, and we'll make some cookies."

Zoe relished her daughter's grin. One that used to flash all the time before the kidnapping attempt a month ago. She'd been walking home from school when a car pulled up beside her. The vehicle door had flown open, and hands had reached for Sophia. Zoe had been standing on the porch watching it, horrified at the possibility that the man would manage to get her daughter into the vehicle. She'd raced toward them screaming for Sophia to run. Sophia had, and the car had squealed away.

Zoe shuddered.

Then the attempt to run Zoe off the road and leave her in the ditch—or worse, have her go over the side of the cliff…

She shook her head.

At least now they were safe until she could figure out whom to trust and ask for help. Running two hundred miles away from Knoxville, Tennessee, to this little town in the middle of nowhere had seemed like a good idea a few weeks ago. Now she wasn't sure.

Oh, the people in town were friendly enough, but she and Sophia were so isolated out here. More isolated than she'd intended or understood it to be when she'd taken the job. She drew in a deep breath. But it served its purpose. "Stop it. Get the water and put your worries behind you. You have a painting to finish," Zoe told herself. She was extremely grateful she could work from anywhere. Her paintings sold well in a variety of shops all over the country, providing a good living for her and Sophia. She looked over the area. If she could live anywhere on a permanent basis, it would be somewhere like this. A rich land with horses to ride and plenty of fresh air to breathe.

"Hey, Mom?"

She turned back to Sophia. "Yes?"

"When is Lily going to have her baby?"

Lily, the pregnant heifer. "Any day now."

"Is Doctor Aaron going to come check on her today?"

At the mention of the hunky veterinarian, Zoe's heart turned a flip. "Yes, he'll be here soon, I imagine."

"I like him." Sophia skipped back to the hose to finish wrapping it.

Yeah, I do, too. She'd run into him at the local diner when he'd walked in with a service animal he had been training. Sophia had been instantly captivated by both man and beast. Zoe hadn't been far behind. When she realized he was the vet who would be checking on Lily on a daily basis, she'd ordered her heart to chill. To no avail. It still did a little happy dance every time he showed up.

She walked up the porch steps and reached for the knob of the door. Only to stop and snatch her hand away.

The door wasn't shut all the way. The black crack from top to bottom mocked her. She stepped back, her pulse ratcheting up several notches.

She knew she'd shut the door. With the indoor cat, who liked to make her escape whenever the opportunity presented itself, Zoe was extra careful with the doors. So why was it open? Had Sophia—

"Mom!"

Sophia's harsh scream spun Zoe around. Her fear spiking, she froze and stumbled a full turn. A large man held Sophia by her ponytail, a gun pointed to her head. Her daughter cried out again and tried to pull away, but he held her easily.

"Let her go!" Zoe moved toward them, her only thought to get her child away from the man.

He moved the weapon so it pointed at Zoe, his finger tightening on the trigger. A cruel smile tilted his thin lips upward. "Bye-bye."

Zoe shook, somehow made her legs work and ducked behind the wheelbarrow just as a loud crack splintered the air. Sophia screamed, a high-pitched, ear-piercing wail full of terror. Zoe's legs gave out and she hit the ground hard. She tried to think, but the horror sweeping over her wouldn't let her. She had to get to Sophia. She had to get her child back.

"Stop, you moron! Don't shoot her!"

Zoe's breath came in pants, her terror lessening a fraction as relief filled her. Someone had come. She nearly sobbed. She forced her legs to stand, to take a step toward the man who still held a crying Sophia. He kept the gun held on Zoe, but glanced at the other man who'd stepped from inside the house, cell phone pressed to his ear. "Don't shoot her!"

Relief fled and fear gripped her again. What was this second man doing in her house? She headed to Sophia who continued to struggle in spite of the pain inflicted by the man's hold on her hair. With his other hand, he aimed the weapon at Zoe, but didn't pull the trigger, his gaze still darting between her and the man behind her. When she was two steps from Sophia, her daughter's eyes widened and her attention focused behind her. Zoe turned to look over her shoulder, saw a flash of movement. Before she had time to think, something crashed into the side of her forehead, pain exploded through her skull and she fell to the ground.

Aaron Starke stepped up to the counter and took the two prescription bags from Lucille Andrews, the pharmacist for the Wrangler's Corner Pharmacy. "Thanks."

"No problem. Hope your mom feels better fast."

"It's just an ear infection. She should be fine in a day or so."

"And thanks for taking that out to Zoe. I know she'll appreciate it."

"Happy to do it. See you later." He headed back to his truck and tossed the bags onto the passenger seat. One for his mother and one for the pretty single mom he couldn't seem to get out of his head. Although he really needed to.

Well, he was going out to the farm anyway to check on the pregnant heifer. Taking the prescription was only being neighborly, nothing else. Right? Right.

Ten minutes later, he turned into the Updikes' drive and followed it up to the main house. A large four-bedroom home, it looked lived-in and loved, with Thanksgiving decorations hung on the door and a small flag with the words "Thankful for Blessings" stuck in the ground. He figured that was Zoe's doing. He didn't remember Martha Updike bothering with that kind of thing.

Aaron coasted to a stop at the top of the drive. An old pickup truck sat in front of him. He'd never seen it before and knew Zoe didn't drive it. She had a Jeep Wrangler. Maybe she had family visiting? Then he noticed the open barn door and frowned. Why would Zoe have the door open when the temperatures were already dropping and were supposed to hit record colds tonight?

He climbed out of the truck and pulled his heavy down coat tighter against his throat. He shoved his hands into his gloves and settled his hat more firmly on his head. Snowflakes drifted down littering the ground that was already starting to turn white. Aaron tromped across the few remaining dried twigs that would be green grass come springtime and knocked on the door. "Zoe? You in there? Sophia? It's Aaron Starke."

He peered inside and all the animals looked well taken care of with fresh water in their buckets and clean stalls. Aaron walked down to the office and unlocked it. He placed Sophia's medication on the desk, left the office and locked it behind him.

His next stop was to check on Lily the pregnant cow. She'd been brought in out of the cold and now stood in one of the horse stalls looking fat and ready to get the whole thing over with. He checked her and found the calf had turned. "Well, that's good news," he told her and gave her bulging belly a light pat.

He cleaned up in the large barn sink then

decided to check on Zoe. He thought it strange she hadn't come out to at least say hi and ask about the cow. She had all the other times he'd been by. And every time he'd seen her and talked to her, he'd wound up leaving with her on his mind. Where she stayed. Constantly. He'd learned a few things about her. She loved her daughter, she was a very private person—and she was worried about something.

Satisfied that all was well in the barn, he left and shut the door behind him. A frigid wind blasted across his face, and he shivered. He headed to the house, his heavy boots crunching the brown grass that would soon be covered in the snow still coming down.

A glint from the ground caught his eye, and he stopped. He stooped down to poke into the dirt and snow with a gloved finger and uncovered a silver necklace with a pretty blue charm. He picked it up, and a red liquid substance slid onto his tan glove. He frowned. Lifted his hand and sniffed. The coppery smell of blood reached him. He spied a large footprint in the area next to the where he'd found the necklace. A boot print too large to be Zoe's.

He looked up, truly concerned for Zoe and

Sophia now. He glanced back at the earth and realized the blood wasn't just limited to that one spot. It trailed drop by drop to the front porch. He followed it, saw more blood on the steps. It could be a simple thing. Maybe she cut her hand on one of the tools in the barn or Sophia fell and scraped her knee or…something.

But the necklace in the dirt bothered him. It hadn't been there long. There was no rust or embedded dirt. And the blood was still fresh.

If it had been just one thing, he might not have been overly concerned, but the open barn door, the necklace, the trail of blood that had only just begun to dry, her car parked in the covered area but no sign of Zoe or Sophia…the boot print.

She was here. Somewhere. The blood suggested close by and in trouble. He moved up onto the wraparound porch and saw more drops of red at the base of the door. He tried to see in the window, but the gauzy curtain blocked his view. Aaron walked around the perimeter of the house and saw nothing else amiss.

He knocked on the door. A scuffling sound came from inside but no one answered. He knocked again. "Zoe? You in there? You okay?"

* * *

Zoe stared up at the man who pointed the weapon at the end of her nose. Her head throbbed, but at least the blood had begun to dry. Fear pounded through her and she couldn't stop shaking. Sophia clung to her and buried her face in Zoe's neck. "Get rid of him," her captor growled. "Now. Or I'll have to shoot him."

"We don't need any more trouble, Pete," the other one muttered from his position by the window. He held the gun loosely in his left hand. Comfortably. As though he used it on a regular basis.

"Like I don't know that," Pete said. The angry scowl twisted his face into something from a horror movie. Zoe wanted to close her eyes and shut them all out, but she couldn't. She kept her arms around Sophia's slight frame. Her daughter was so little, so vulnerable.

"Now, I said." He jabbed the gun at her, and Zoe flinched. She glanced at the door and back at the man who'd intervened and saved her only to hold her and Sophia captive. She rose on shaky legs, stumbled then caught herself. Sophia rose with her, refusing to let go. Zoe's head swam and bile climbed into her throat. She breathed deep and the dizziness settled.

The man called Pete grabbed Sophia by the arm and jerked her away from Zoe. Sophia cried out. Pete slapped a hand across her mouth. "Make another sound and I'll shoot your mother, you understand?"

Zoe stood frozen, wanting to smash the man's face in, but knew one wrong move could cause him to hurt her daughter. "It's okay, honey, just sit still for a minute, all right?" she said.

Sophia's gaze clung to hers, but she gave a small nod. Pete relaxed his grip a fraction, and Sophia didn't move even as silent tears tracked a path down her ashen cheeks.

"Hey, Zoe? You okay? It's Aaron Starke. I came to check on Lily and wanted to say hi." The pounding on the front door resumed, and she walked over to it.

The man near the window lifted his weapon, an unneeded reminder that he was watching. Zoe closed her eyes and drew in a desperately needed calming breath, praying for strength—and some way to convey the fact that she needed help without putting the person at the door in harm's way.

With one last glance at Sophia, she pulled on every ounce of inner strength, ignored the throbbing in her head and opened the door. Aaron stood on the front porch. His large frame filled the doorway, blocking the icy wind and the sunlight. He had to be half a foot taller than her own five foot eight. She forced a trembling smile to her lips. "Hi."

He offered a frown in response. "I came by to check on that pregnant heifer and saw some blood on the ground and a necklace. This yours?" He held it out to her as his gaze landed on her right temple.

"Um. Yes. Thanks." She took it and stuffed it in her front pocket.

He leaned in to take a closer look. "What happened? That looks like a pretty bad gash."

She raised a shaky hand to lightly touch the wound. "Oh, that." A laugh slipped out, but it sounded nervous to her ears. Scared. She shifted her weight from one foot to the other and her eyes darted away from his only to return a fraction of a second later. "I was… ah…clumsy, tripped over the water hose in the barn and hit the side of the stall. I was just getting ready to clean the wound when you knocked."

"Why don't I give you a hand? I'm pretty good at that kind of thing. Granted, most of my patients are of the four-legged variety, but the concept is the same." He moved as though to enter and panic filled her.

She shifted and blocked his entrance. "Really, I'm fine. I can do it."

He paused, his eyes probing the area behind her. She knew he couldn't see anything but the stairs that led up to the second floor. "Well. Okay. If you're sure." He backed up, his boots clunking on the wooden porch.

No! she wanted to scream. She widened her eyes and cut them to the side window. *Don't leave!*

But he simply tapped his hat in a gentlemanly gesture and turned to go. Then spun back. Her breath caught. Had he figured out she needed help? Did he know someone stood behind her with a gun? "Oh, by the way," he said, "I was in the pharmacy a little bit ago getting a prescription for my mother and Mrs. Lucille gave me Sophia's medication. I left it on the desk in the office in the barn."

"Oh, th-thank you. We were getting low."

"I'll just go get it for you."

"No, no, that's okay, I can get it. I'm going to have to go out there and…ah…fill the water buckets anyway."

He tilted his head and gave a slow nod. "All right then. Holler if you need anything."

She nodded but couldn't force any more

words out of her tight, tear-filled throat. This time when he turned around, he didn't look back. She shut the door with a soft snick and turned to find the two men staring at her.

Pete let go of Sophia and she rushed at Zoe, wrapping her arms around her waist and holding tight. Zoe met Pete's gaze since he seemed to be the one in charge. "Now what?" she whispered. "What do you want?"

His eyes dropped to Sophia. "Her."

TWO

That niggling feeling wouldn't leave him alone. Aaron sat in his truck outside the house, but didn't crank it. Instead he dialed Lance Goode's personal cell number. Lance was a deputy with the Wrangler's Corner sheriff's department and a good friend of the Starke family. Aaron's brother, Clay, the sheriff, was out of town until later that evening so the safety of Wrangler's Corner fell on Lance's shoulders. The deputy answered on the second ring. "Hello?"

"How far are you from the Updike farm?"

"Not too far. Why?"

"Something weird's going on here."

"Aren't the Updikes out of town?"

"Yeah." The curtain on the window by the door fluttered. He cranked his truck and debated whether or not to drive off. "But Zoe Collier and her daughter, Sophia, are staying here while the Updikes are on their cruise. I just knocked on the door and she answered, but she had a gash on her head that she said she got from falling against the side of the barn."

"You have reason to doubt her?"

"No, not really, but she just looked… scared. And she said something about having to go out there and fill up the water buckets. I was just in the barn, Lance. The buckets are full of fresh water and the hose is neatly wrapped and hanging on the reel."

Lance made a noise low in his throat. "That does sound kind of odd. If she hit her head, she might have a concussion or something. Be a little confused."

"Maybe. She didn't seem confused, just scared."

"All right. I'm on my way. It's probably nothing but I'll come check it out."

"Thanks. I guess I'll head on back to the office." Aaron hung up and put his truck in gear. His secretary, Janice Maynard, was out on maternity leave and his partner was on vacation for the next three days.

Managing by himself was a huge headache, and he should have listened to his father's advice about hiring a temporary person to fill in, but then he'd have the headache of training the person. He grimaced. He still hadn't decided which choice was the lesser of the two evils. Regardless, he didn't like to stay gone too long. Then again, that was one of the advantages of living in a small town. Everyone had his cell number and if someone needed him, they'd call.

Aaron drove down the drive and out of sight of the house then stopped at the base of a sloping hill. He tapped his fingers on the wheel. He couldn't do it. He couldn't just leave. There'd been something in her eyes when she'd looked at him then cut her eyes toward the left. Had someone been there? Someone she'd been afraid off? What if an abusive ex had found her or something? Or what if she really did have a concussion? He didn't remember seeing any sign of one when he'd looked into her green eyes, but he hadn't been looking for one, either. Had her pupils been even?

He grunted. Nope. He couldn't leave. Aaron turned the vehicle around and drove back up to the house. He parked next to the strange truck and shut the engine off. He hesitated only a second before he opened the driver's door and stepped out. He stared at the other truck, walked over to it and looked inside. Fast food wrappers and cigarette butts littered the cab, but nothing that set off any alarms. He sighed and marched back up to the front door. Before he could knock, the door opened and he found himself staring down the barrel of a gun.

Aaron froze. Now his internal alarms were ringing. Okay, he'd thought she'd looked scared, but this wasn't what he'd pictured. The angry dark eyes behind the gun glittered. "Get in here, hero. You had your chance to leave, but guess you get to join the fun."

Zoe wanted to weep. Her only hope of rescue had just joined them as a hostage. Aaron lifted his hands in the surrender position and walked into the house. His eyes landed on her and Sophia, huddled together on the couch. She knew she probably looked terrified as she locked her gaze on his. Well, that was fine. She *was* terrified.

Aaron moved closer to them, putting his body between her and Sophia and the gun. The other man, whose name she hadn't learned yet, shut the door behind Aaron. "What's going on?"

"Just taking care of a little business is all. Now hand over your cell phone and your weapon."

"I'm a veterinarian. What makes you think I have a weapon?"

Pete laughed without a smidge of humor. "You don't live in this kind of town and *not* carry a weapon." His hard eyes turned to chips. "Hand it over."

Aaron didn't bother to protest, just pulled his .38 special from his shoulder holster and gave it to the man. When he did, his keys fell to the floor.

"I'll take those, too. No sense in giving you something that could poke an eye out." Aaron hesitated then snagged his cell phone from the clip on his belt and released that, as well. From her position behind him, she could see the tension in the set of his shoulders and prayed he didn't do anything that would cause one of the men to shoot him. Or her. "What kind of business?" Aaron asked.

"Shut up." Pete looked at his partner. "Now what?"

"Tie him up," the partner said. He eyed Aaron. "Anyone know you're here?"

"Several people know I'm coming out here on a regular basis to check on one of the heifers ready to deliver any day now." He stayed still while Pete used duct tape to secure his hands behind him.

The partner shoved the gun at him. "Let me rephrase the question. Anyone know you're here right now?"

"No, but when I don't show up for dinner, my family will be looking for me."

Zoe stayed still, listening, feeling Sophia's heart beat against her side. Her rapid heartbeat. Zoe looked closer and saw the sweat on her daughter's forehead. She lifted Sophia's chin and looked in her eyes. She stood. "My daughter needs some food."

"Shut up and sit down," the partner said without taking his eyes from Aaron.

Zoe stayed put. "My child needs sugar in her system. She has diabetes. Her sugar is dropping, and I need to give her something sweet. Now." She tried to keep her voice steady and firm. She failed miserably on the steady part. She lifted her chin and met Pete's eyes when he finally turned them on her. "She could die and while I don't think you care if I do, for some reason you want her alive."

The man's eyes narrowed, and he stared at her as though trying to figure out if she was telling the truth or not.

Zoe wanted to scream. Instead, she clamped down on her emotions and pointed at Sophia. "Look at her. Sweating, rapid pulse, lethargy. If we don't regulate her blood sugar, she could faint and go into a coma."

For a moment he simply studied her. "Fine.

Get her something, but Cody's going to be watching you. You try to get a knife or something, and you'll pay, you understand?"

"I understand. I just want to get her some orange juice." Zoe turned to Sophia. "Stay right here. I'll be back in a second."

"No, Mom—"

"Shh. You need some sugar. Do as I say, sweetie." She tried to comfort Sophia while watching the man with the gun. His impatience escalated, and she backed toward the kitchen. Sophia's lower lip trembled.

Aaron moved closer to Sophia. "It'll be a bit awkward, but you can hold my hand, honey. Your mom will be right back."

Sophia's eyes darted back and forth between her mother and Aaron, and she nodded. Zoe suspected she was feeling a bit dizzy as she simply laid her head against the back of the couch and shut her eyes.

Zoe moved toward the kitchen, not wanting to leave Sophia, but knowing the man beside her baby was an honorable one—at least according to everything she'd heard about him during the short time she'd been in town—and wouldn't let anyone hurt Sophia if at all possible.

Zoe acted fast. She could feel Cody's eyes on her, watching, waiting for her to make a wrong move. She grabbed the orange juice from the refrigerator and a glass from the cabinet. Her hands were shaking so hard she was afraid she'd spill the liquid. She stopped for a second and took a calming breath.

Then she picked up the carton and poured the juice into the glass. Sophia didn't usually have a problem with her diabetes when she ate right, got her exercise and did what she was supposed to do, but it had been a stressful few weeks and her body was reacting to it. This situation definitely wasn't helping.

Zoe hurried back into the den and over to Sophia. "Here, honey, drink this."

Sophia wrapped her hand around the glass while Zoe helped her. Her daughter drank the juice while Zoe's eyes met Aaron's. His shoulders gave a slight twitch, and she realized he was using her as a shield while he worked on getting his hands free. She stood over Sophia for as long as she dared then turned to find their two captors in conversation. Discussing how to kill them? Bitterness welled and she tamped it down. *God, get us out of this, please.*

"Sit down," Pete said and jabbed her with his weapon.

Aaron stilled, and Zoe sat beside Sophia who seemed to already be doing better with the juice. Zoe set the glass on the table then turned back to Sophia. She ran a hand over her daughter's face and pulled her close. Pete and his partner, the one he called Cody, moved to look out the window then went back to their discussion. Aaron leaned closer. "What do they want?" he whispered.

"I don't know." She wasn't going to tell him what the man had said about wanting Sophia. Not while her daughter was listening to every word.

"How many are there?" Aaron asked.

"I've only seen the two."

Pete turned a sharp eye in their direction, and she snapped her mouth shut then leaned over to kiss the top of Sophia's head. A ringing phone broke the tense stillness.

Pete turned away to answer, and Cody disappeared out the door. "Lance is on his way out here," Aaron said, his voice so low she had to strain to hear it. Pete bent his head and muttered something into the phone. "He may be here already."

"Who's Lance?"

"A deputy sheriff. I called him and told him something was wrong out here. He said he'd head over and check it out."

Hope blossomed and she prayed.

"I got my hands free," he whispered. "Sit

tight. Better do this while there's only one. While I distract Pete, you grab Sophia and run."

"Don't—"

Pete hung up and walked back into the den. "Looks like we're stuck here a bit longer."

"What are you waiting for?" Aaron asked.

"Instructions."

He turned slightly, and Aaron sprang from the couch. He slammed into Pete, and they both went to the floor. Sophia screamed, and Zoe clutched her close. Aaron grunted as a fist caught him across the cheek. Zoe looked for a weapon she could use to help. Aaron rolled, avoiding another fist in the face. "Run, Zoe!"

Zoe pushed Sophia toward the front door. "Go. Run as fast as you can into the trees. Hide until you hear me calling. I'll find you." She wanted her child safe, but she wasn't going to leave Aaron to fight alone.

Sophia ran for the door and unlocked it. Zoe grabbed a vase from the end table next to the sofa.

The back door crashed in and a deputy stepped into the kitchen. She could see him assessing the situation in a lightning-fast second. He moved through the small hall into the den and aimed his weapon at the men on the floor. "Police! Freeze!"

Aaron rammed a punch into Pete's gut, and the man gasped, rolled to his knees and put his head on the floor.

Aaron stumbled back. Sophia froze near the front door then ran back to Zoe who set the vase back onto the table and gathered her child close.

Lance moved quickly and cuffed the man on the floor while Aaron went to the window to peer out. "There's another one. He left just a minute ago."

The front door slammed open.

Zoe gasped and spun to find Cody and yet a third man standing there with weapons aimed at them. Lance lifted his gun and aimed it at the two men. "Drop your weapons."

The third man stepped closer. "I don't think so." He simply shifted his gun so that it was pointed at Sophia. "Now everyone is going to settle down." His gaze darted between Lance, Aaron and the man on the ground. He came back to Lance. "Lose your weapon and your phone and uncuff Pete." Lance glared but didn't argue, placing his gun and cell phone on the table with the others. Aaron sank back onto the couch, dabbing his bruised cheek.

The newcomer waited until Pete was on his feet before he spoke. "Thought you said you had him tied up."

"He was," Pete grunted with a scowl.

"Tape him up again. Put his hands in front of him so we can see what he's doing with them." He flicked a glance at Lance. "Both of them."

Despair welled in Zoe as Aaron and Lance submitted to having their hands bound in front of them. She wanted to wail in frustration. They'd been so close. So very close. She huddled with Sophia and prayed—in spite of the fact that she was convinced that God didn't care what happened to those she loved.

THREE

Pete got up from the floor and turned his dark eyes on Aaron. The venom there sent a cold shiver of fear through him. And certain knowledge that Pete wanted to kill him. Aaron figured if the man got his hands on a gun, it would all be over. Aaron had made an enemy for life. One he'd better not ever let have access to his back. He felt sure he could take the man in a one-on-one fight, but Aaron knew he was no match with bound hands. He kept his gaze steady, refusing to flinch. Finally Pete looked away, grabbed his weapon from the floor and aimed it at Aaron.

"Put it away, Pete," the newcomer ordered.

"But Jed—"

"Now. There'll be time for revenge later." Aaron didn't like the fact that the man could speak without raising his voice and the two men did as ordered. Jed turned his gaze to the blond man. "Cody, get on the phone and find out what the problem is. We can't stay here forever. Start the truck and once we're away from here we'll figure out what to do with them."

Cody tossed his shaggy blond hair out of his eyes and snagged his phone from the back pocket of his jeans. He punched in a number, shot them all a vicious look and backed out the door. Aaron glanced at Lance who'd also placed himself in a protective stance between the men and Zoe and Sophia. A cold feeling had settled in the pit of Aaron's stomach. These men didn't think anything about using each other's names. Because they didn't plan on anyone being able to tell who they were?

Pete stepped forward and taped Lance's hands together then gave him a shove onto the couch. Lance landed with a grunt beside Zoe.

When Pete moved his attention to him, Aaron looked at the new guy who'd displaced Cody with his authority. Jed. "Look, if I don't check in with my family, they're going to come looking for me."

"Shut up."

"My brother is the sheriff of this town," Aaron continued softly. "Unless you want him on the doorstep as well, you'll let me text him and let him know I'm going to be busy all night delivering that calf out in the barn. I also have some medication for my mother I picked up at the pharmacy. My dad's going to be calling and wondering why I haven't dropped it off yet."

Jed's eyes narrowed and he cut a glance at Pete. Aaron turned his attention to him. "And in case you're wondering, I don't want my family coming here and stumbling into this mess. I'm not trying to put something over on you. I'm actually just trying to keep my family away from you. Less trouble for you, too, if no one else shows up." Might as well say it like it is. Even then, there wasn't any guarantee that Clay wouldn't come by to check on him or take it upon himself to come get their mother's medicine, but with Sabrina due to deliver their first child any day now, he figured Clay would stay pretty close to home once he got back from his trip. Which meant he might send someone. Either way it would involve putting someone else in danger if he didn't let them hear from him.

Jed eyed him. "Fine." He jutted his chin at Pete. "Text what he tells you."

Pete's eyes narrowed, but he found Aaron's phone. "You've got four new texts."

"Like I said, better let me answer them, or

I'll have people looking for me." He met Pete's gaze. "And they know where to find me."

Pete looked to his boss for confirmation. The man nodded. "Who and what do I text?"

Aaron gave instructions, not even trying to insert a hidden message in his words. It would be too obvious anyway. He added. "One more. Text to my dad, 'Calf due to deliver any moment. Won't have time to drop off Mom's meds. See if Doc Whaley will give her two pills to tide her over till I can get there probably tomorrow.'"

When the messages had been sent, he allowed Pete to duct-tape his hands together once again. One less thing to worry about. His family wouldn't come out to the farm and find themselves in danger. He sat back on the sofa while the other two men paced and muttered and checked their phones. They were waiting on something. Orders from someone?

Cody stomped back into the house, flakes of snow melting in his hair, blistering curses on his lips. "I gotta go into town and get a part. The truck won't start."

"What? What happened?" Jed asked.

"I don't know. I think it's a spark plug."

"Take mine." Jed tossed Cody his keys. "Don't be long."

"Guess I'll be as long as it takes."

At Jed's cold stare, Cody ducked his head. "But it won't take long." He trudged back out, and Aaron heard the vehicle start up and drive away.

He turned his attention to the boss. "You mind if I check on the heifer out in the barn?"

A heavy sigh slipped from the man. "You mind if I put a bullet through your head?"

A whimper escaped Sophia, and Aaron's fingers flexed into fists. He forced himself to relax. "Come on, man, it's an animal." He gestured to Zoe and Sophia and Lance. "As long as you have them, I'm not going to do anything stupid."

Jed studied him then nodded to Pete. "Fine. Go with him."

"What?"

The two exchanged a silent look. "Go with him," Jed repeated.

Pete lifted a brow. "Right." He shot Aaron a grim smile. "Let's go."

Aaron figured that exchange between the partners was permission for Pete to kill him. His heart thudded a faster beat, and he sent up prayers for safety and wisdom. Truly all he'd wanted was to get in the barn and deliver the calf should the mama be ready. Now, it appeared he was going to have to fight for his life.

Zoe didn't miss the interaction between the three men. She jumped up. "I'll go with you. You might need some help." Then she stopped. She wasn't leaving Sophia behind, though. "Sophia's a great help in the barn, as well."

"This isn't some country club vacation!" Pete yelled. "Sit down and shut up!"

Zoe sat, and Sophia buried her face in her side with a low cry. Zoe pressed a hand against the little girl's head, trying to offer comfort. "Shh…"

"I'll be fine," Aaron said. "Just do what they say."

She bit her lip. "But—"

"Don't argue, Zoe," Lance said. She frowned. Sophia pulled on her hand, so she snapped her lips shut.

Pete followed Aaron out the door and Zoe couldn't help the prayers that slipped from her lips. She looked at Jed. "What do you want? Why are you doing this?" She glanced at his phone. "Who are you waiting for? Who's supposed to call?"

He waved the weapon at her. "You just need to be quiet. You've led us on a merry chase."

"Was it you who tried to kidnap Sophia

from her school?" She regretted the question when his gaze slid from her to Sophia. He didn't answer. *"Why?"*

"Shut up!"

Lance reached over with his hands taped together at the wrist, and clasped her fingers in a light squeeze. Zoe clamped her lips closed. Lance sat so quiet she'd almost forgotten about him. She shot him a frantic glance. Jed's phone rang, and he stepped back still keeping an eye on them as he answered. As soon as he averted his gaze, she leaned toward Lance. "He's going to kill Aaron," she whispered. "We have to do something."

Sophia's arms tightened around her at her words, but she couldn't just sit there and let Aaron die.

"Aaron has a plan," Lance said. "I could see it in his eyes. Let's let him play it out."

"What if it backfires? What if he needs help?"

"I know Aaron, he'll be all right."

Zoe saw the worry in his eyes and wondered if he really believed it or was just trying to ease her mind. She feared the latter. "But—"

"Hey! Zip it!" Jed's shout made her flinch, and she blinked back a surge of tears. Lance's hand stayed clamped around hers and she sank back against the couch even as she looked for a way to secure a weapon—or something to release Lance's hands with.

Aaron went straight to his truck and pulled his vet bag from the passenger seat. It was awkward with his hands taped, but he managed. Pete didn't say anything, just watched him. Aaron ignored him and headed for the barn, his mind spinning. *God, help me, please. Don't let him kill me. Let me be ready to fight back when he strikes.*

Once inside he went to Lily's stall and saw the heifer pacing. The area had been extended so it was double the size of a normal stall. Lily lay down then got up. After repeating this for several minutes, she finally stayed down. She lowed, a painful groan that Aaron knew would grow in intensity in the next few minutes.

Aaron looked at Pete. "I need my hands. She's ready."

"Not a chance."

With his hands still taped in front of him, Aaron got the heater and turned it on. He placed it in the stall and watched the heifer get up then lie down again. This time she let out a loud bellow that shook the rafters of the barn.

Pete watched him, his dark eyes hard. Cold. His right hand held his weapon in an easy grip. His finger played with the trigger.

Aaron gave a shudder as fear swept through him. But he kept his cool. He had to. Zoe, Sophia and Lance were probably going to need him. The gun swung up. A Glock.

All it would take to end his life was the twitch of the man's finger. "If you kill me before she delivers, this cow is going to put up such a holler she'll bring the neighbors down on you." As if to confirm his words the heifer let out another moan. Louder this time than the last.

Pete frowned then scoffed. "What neighbors?"

"There's the Garrett farm to the left and the Hunt farm to the right." He lifted his chin to the north. "Up that way just behind the tree line, there's a pretty big general store. The owner is there every day and he'll hear the cow bawling if I don't deliver this calf. The owner of the store is Michael Richardson and a good friend of the Updikes. He'll be here within minutes to find out what's going on. You want that?"

Aaron's words seemed to sink in. Pete cursed and spit on the ground, but at least he removed the gun from Aaron's face. "I saw that store. Stopped to get gas there. Dude asked twenty questions and wouldn't shut up about wondering who I was visiting and spending the holidays with." He scowled.

"Yep, that's Michael." He paused. "Or you can kill me, I guess, and deliver the calf yourself." The heifer chose that moment to make her presence known with a screeching groan that morphed into a low grunt. Pete flinched, his eyes darting to the barn door as though he expected someone to start pounding on them at any second. "At least if I'm here if someone shows up," Aaron said, "I'll be able to reassure them that everything's all right." He met Pete's gaze. "Trust me, I don't want anyone hurt. If someone shows up, I'll make sure they think everything is just fine."

The heifer bellowed again.

"Or I could just shoot her."

Aaron winced. "Yeah, you could. And again, bring attention to the fact you're here. True, this is the country and people carry guns. And use them. But we're mostly civilized and neighbors around here still respond to gunshots."

"No one came when I shot at that pretty little lady in there."

"You're fortunate. You want to push it?"

Still glaring, Pete pulled a large knife from

his front pocket and flipped it open. "Guess I could just use this then."

Aaron winced. "Yes, I supposed you could." He sighed. "Come on, man, let me deliver the calf and be done with it."

Pete hesitated, and Aaron really didn't like the look in the man's eyes. The cow groaned, and Pete muttered a few choice words. He leaned toward Aaron, and Aaron braced himself, expecting to feel the knife sink into his flesh.

One swipe was all it took to split the tape holding Aaron's hands together. Aaron hissed as the blood rushed to his fingers and he flexed them even while his brain scrambled for an escape route. He needed to do something and fast before Cody came back—or Pete decided to throw caution to the wind and exact his revenge.

He looked at Lily. She hadn't gotten up again so she was definitely ready. At least the barn was warm. The heater was a heavy-duty propane deal that put out enough warmth to keep the stall nice and toasty. A plan began to form even as he shrugged out of his coat. He maneuvered his way around to the heifer and rubbed her head to reassure her. She knew him and didn't seem nervous around him. Aaron prayed for an easy birth. Her moaning and bellowing continued. He looked up to see Pete had moved closer, his hard eyes flat. Waiting. Every so often they would flick toward the door. Good. Aaron's words had him thinking someone would show up.

Aaron knew as soon as he delivered the calf he was dead. While he worked with the mama and baby, he thought, planned and prayed. He pulled the calving chains from the bag he'd dropped on the ground. Pete lifted the gun. "What are you doing?"

"They're to help pull the calf out if I need them. I might not, but I need to have them nearby."

Pete stayed silent, but watchful.

Aaron worked with the heifer, soothing her and rubbing her belly, feeling the baby move. Thankfully, it wasn't breech any longer. It had turned the right way and from here on out, the heifer would do most of the work. Aaron would assist while he went through the plan over and over in his head.

Finally, after a number of hard contractions and bellows from the soon-to-be mama, he saw the calf's legs poking out and slipped on a clean pair of gloves to help the baby out into the world. "Hand me those chains, would you?"

"I'm not here to help."

That's what he figured the man would say. Aaron gritted his teeth and left the chains on the bag. He didn't really need them anyway. He wrapped his hands around the baby's legs and heard the heifer give another moan, waited on the next contraction, then pulled. While the mother let out one last bellowing yell, the calf slipped onto the fresh hay and Aaron worked to clear its nose. He then teased a nostril with a piece of straw to make it sneeze. It obliged and Aaron went to work on the afterbirth. Once he had everything finished, he rolled his head and glanced at his captor from the corner of his eye.

Pete had moved closer, the gun now trained on Aaron. Aaron casually pulled the gloves from his hands and dumped them in the trash bag he'd brought out.

He stood as though to stretch, but instead, in one smooth move, spun, grabbed the heater and swung it around into Pete's head. The man didn't even cry out. He simply slumped to the ground, the weapon landing with a thump on the hay. Aaron grabbed the calving chains and tied the man up. Heart pounding, adrenaline surging, he stood back and looked at his handiwork. A long gash in the man's head bled freely, but Aaron didn't think he'd done too much damage. And Pete might manage to get out of the chains eventually, but it would take him a bit of time. Hopefully, he and the others would be long gone by then and law enforcement would have things under control.

Breathing heavily, Aaron pulled Pete from the stall then went back and grabbed his coat. He shoved his hands into the sleeves, grabbed Pete's gun, then slipped back out of the stall shutting the mama and baby in behind him. He stuck Pete's gun in his shoulder holster.

A phone, he needed a phone.

He patted the man down, searched his pockets and came up empty. Great. There was a phone in the office.

He raced to it and twisted the knob. Locked. And he didn't have his keys. Aaron stepped back, lifted a foot and kicked. The door shook, but held. Three more kicks and it swung open. He grabbed the handset from the base and turned it on. Listened.

To nothing.

He groaned. They'd cut the landline.

He stopped and pressed a hand against his forehead. *Think, think. Consider your options.*

And came up with one.

Overpower Jed, get the others out before Cody came back. Or Pete woke up. It wasn't a great plan—or even a plan at all—it was just what he knew he had to do.

Aaron slipped out of the barn and up to the house. He figured boss man would be in the den or at least near it to keep an eye on Lance, Zoe and Sophia. He'd go in the front door as he figured it was probably still unlocked. His rushing adrenaline made him shaky and clumsy. He took a deep breath. He wasn't a cop, this wasn't his deal. He was perfectly happy to leave catching the bad guys and rescuing people to Clay and the deputies, but today it fell to him.

He wanted to hurry, but had to be careful. If he got caught this time, there wouldn't be a third chance for escape. They didn't need him as Pete had just proven while in the barn. He and Lance were collateral damage. He couldn't believe Pete had bought his story about neighbors coming to check on the cow. Most likely, they'd have heard her and figured she was giving birth and Aaron was there to help. Birth was a noisy affair, and the neighbors knew that. Aaron's hunch that Pete wouldn't know that had paid off.

At the front door, he paused, placed a hand on the knob and twisted slowly. Nothing happened, so he cracked it enough to see inside.

The foyer, the living area to the left, dining to the right. The den was straight ahead. He slipped inside and shut the door behind him.

He listened, ear tuned to the slightest sound, muscles bunched and ready to act. Sounded like Jed was on the phone. He glanced out the window and thought he saw a vehicle down the drive. Cody coming back?

Heart racing, he moved until he could see Lance still on the couch with Zoe. Sophia sat between them. He caught Lance's eye. Lance blinked but made no other indication that he'd seen Aaron.

"Fine. I'll take care of it. I'll deliver them both tonight. And you'd better have the rest of my money."

Aaron raised the gun.

Lance shifted. "Hey, when are we going to get something to eat? Sophia needs some food even if you're not going to feed the rest of us."

Jed stepped into view, the back of his head toward Aaron. He pointed to Zoe. "Go fix something."

Zoe moved to stand when Aaron stepped up behind Jed and placed his gun against the man's head. "Move and you die." The man froze. "Put the weapon on the counter." Jed did. With his free hand, Aaron took the gun and held it. He nodded to Zoe. "Cut Lance loose."

She raced into the kitchen and came back with a knife. She cut the tape and Lance stood. Jed twitched like he wanted to try something. Aaron pressed the gun harder. "Don't." The man stilled.

"Hey, Jed, Pete? I got the part," Cody called as the back door slammed behind him.

FOUR

Zoe froze, but didn't have time to stand there for long. Jed started to call out, but Lance's fist shot out and caught him in the jaw. Aaron brought the gun down on the back of his head for good measure and the man crumpled to the floor. Lance took the gun from Aaron. "Get them out of here. I'll deal with Cody."

But Cody appeared in the small hallway between the kitchen and the den before Lance could get there. Cody stood for a brief moment, his jaw swinging as he took in the scene, but Zoe didn't stop in her rush to get Sophia out of the house. She reached the large bookcase next to the front door and pulled Sophia next to it praying it was out of the line of fire. She could feel her child's body trembling, but she never made a sound.

"Hey!" She saw Cody's hand lift, the gun aimed at Lance. Lance dropped and rolled in front of the counter and out of sight. Aaron fired his weapon and she saw Cody spin into the wall then hit the floor. Zoe moved away from the bookcase and toward the door, pulling Sophia with her. She looked back to see Cody roll and bring his weapon up again, firing even as Lance aimed at him and pulled the trigger. She dropped to the floor covering Sophia's body with hers. The loud cracks made her ears ring.

"I'm going to kill you! All of you! I don't care about the money anymore, you're all dead!" Pete's bellow came from the kitchen somewhere behind Cody. She heard the door slam once again. Lance leveled his weapon toward the kitchen and fired back. She wanted to get Sophia out, but was afraid to move. Afraid it would be the wrong direction and one of them would catch a bullet. She heard a curse and saw Jed move, shake his head then sit up.

Then Aaron was beside her grabbing Sophia from her and pushing her toward the door. "Go, go, go."

Zoe, Aaron and Sophia raced through the front door. Aaron snagged Sophia's heavy coat as he passed it. Bullets pelted the doorframe, and Sophia screamed. Zoe just followed expecting to feel the slam of a bullet at any moment. Lance was backing out behind them, firing back, keeping the three men at bay.

"Head for the trees!" Aaron urged her. "Don't look back, just run. I've got Sophia."

"Go!" Lance hollered as he whipped around and fired his gun once again. She heard a harsh scream from one of their pursuers but didn't turn. Five more steps and they'd be in the shelter of the trees. The house had been built with a plan to utilize the wooded area for shade during the summer months. Even stripped of most of the leaves, the trees would offer them the most protection. The frigid wind made her flinch, but she couldn't stop now.

Zoe raced into the thicket and turned to find Aaron carrying Sophia in his arms. Lance brought up the rear. He continued to look over his shoulder as they ran. "They're still coming."

"At least they're not shooting," she panted.

"I got one of them, I think. The one they called Jed. Just winged him, though." Lance stayed close. "Keep going. We're going to follow the tree line all the way around and head up to the store on the hill. Hopefully Michael is there and will have a phone we can use."

"Won't they think of that?" Zoe asked.

"Yeah," Aaron grunted. "I basically told

Pete about the place when I was trying to convince him to let my hands free. If we head up there, we'll just put Michael in danger."

Zoe kept casting glances at Sophia. "You okay honey?"

"Just scared," came her small voice.

They kept moving in the direction of the store. "I don't want to put Michael in danger," Zoe said. A shot cracked a tree in front of her.

"Run," Lance ordered.

"Run where?" Aaron grunted, but picked up the pace. "The caves." He answered his own question.

"Yeah, good idea. The caves," Lance said. "Go."

Aaron didn't hesitate, just made a forty-five degree turn and forged a trail for Zoe to follow. Lance brought up the rear. Aaron sloshed through a shallow creek, and Zoe followed, gasping when the cold water hit her legs, but she didn't stop. She could get warm later. Prayers winged heavenward. Weakness wanted to invade her, and she stumbled. Aaron snagged her elbow with one hand even as he kept a grip on Sophia with his other.

Aaron passed the first cave they came to, skirted around brush and trees then simply disappeared. Zoe skidded to a stop. Lance passed her, grasped her hand and pulled her behind him. When he stopped, she found herself in a cave. And cold. So very cold. She couldn't feel her feet anymore. Shivers racked her as Lance stayed at the entrance, his weapon ready. Aaron set Sophia on her feet then helped her into her coat. Sophia let him, but when he stepped back, she moved to Zoe and wrapped her arms around her waist. "I'm scared, Mom," she whispered.

"I am, too, honey, but God's taking care of us."

Sophia looked back and forth between Lance and Aaron. "Yes, I think you're right."

"Now we just have to find a way to call for help," Aaron muttered.

Sophia slipped a hand into the front pocket of her jeans and pulled out a cell phone. "Will this help?"

Aaron stepped up to them, took the phone from Sophia's small hand and looked at the screen. It had about a half battery life, but only one bar. Once out of the cave, he knew there would be a better signal. "Where did you get this?" he whispered.

"That really mean man you called Pete left it on the end table after he tied up Deputy Lance," she said, keeping her voice as low as his and pointing to Lance.

"So you snagged it, huh?"

"Yes." She shrugged. "I was going to try and call 911, but I couldn't do it without someone seeing me so I was just waiting until I could either do it myself or give one of you guys the phone. But that never happened so I just held on to it."

Aaron blinked. "Nice job," he whispered. "Are you sure you're nine?"

"Pretty sure," she whispered back and shot him a weak grin.

Zoe lifted a hand to push Sophia's hair out of her eyes. He noticed the fine tremors racking her and figured she was just as cold as he was.

He punched in the number of the police department and held the phone to his ear on the off chance it would work. The call dropped. He looked at Zoe. "Need a signal."

She nodded and shivered. "Try a text. Sometimes a text will go through when a call won't."

Aaron did. He shrugged. "It says it went, but I don't know if it did or not. We need to make a call. Lance," he whispered.

"Yeah?" Lance turned to face him.

Aaron slipped up beside him and handed him the phone. Lance's eyes went wide. "Thank Sophia," Aaron said.

Lance blinked then gave a tight smile. "Good going, kid."

Sophia nodded. "You're welcome."

Lance went back to the entrance of the cave, and Sophia snuggled next to her mom. Zoe shuddered and pulled her closer. Zoe hadn't had a coat on inside the house and she hadn't had time to grab it before their dash for safety. Now she just had on a sweatshirt over a black turtleneck, and her jeans were soaked to the knees. Aaron shrugged out of his heavy down coat and draped it around her shoulders. She frowned at him. "Thanks, but don't you need it?"

"I'm fine. I worked up a sweat running with Sophia in my arms."

She hesitated then nodded. "If you're sure, I'll just use it to warm up a bit then give it back."

"I'll let you know if I need it."

Their whispers barely sounded in the darkness. The chill of the cave hit him hard, but he wasn't going to let her know that. He hoped they wouldn't be staying put very long anyway. Lance walked back to them. "I think they've passed us. I'm going to slip out of the cave and see if I can get a signal."

Aaron nodded, and Lance again returned to the entrance then disappeared outside. Sophia snuggled in between him and Zoe, and Aaron wrapped his arms around them, pulling them close to share body heat. The cave wall was cold, and the chill seeped through his sweater.

Within seconds, Sophia's head rolled against his chest and her breathing became even. "She fell asleep," he whispered in Zoe's ear.

"Unbelievable. Well, it's been an ordeal between the attack and the diabetes. She's feeling the effects." She froze. "I don't have her medicine," she whispered. "I didn't have time to grab it."

"In the right-hand pocket of my jacket. I snagged it from the office after I knocked Pete out."

Zoe let out a low breath. "Thank you so much." She turned toward him, but shot a glance over her shoulder. "Do you think Lance is all right?"

"I hope so. I don't think he would have left the cave if he thought the men were still out there. It looks like all three of them managed to survive the shots. I think I winged the one called Cody, but it wasn't enough to stop him."

"So it's still three of them."

"Looks like it." He gently shifted Sophia

until she rested against Zoe. "Hold her. I'm going to check on him."

"Be careful," she whispered. "Oh, you need your coat."

"I'll be fine. Stay put."

He moved before she could voice the protest he saw on her lips.

As he moved to the entrance of the cave, a shot rang out, and Lance dove inside.

Sophia woke with a jerk, and Zoe held her even as her own heartbeat picked up speed. "Why are they shooting again, Mama?"

"I don't know, honey, just be brave."

Lance knelt on the floor and looked back at her then Aaron. "I got a call out, but help's a good ten minutes away. Even then I'm not sure they'll be able to pinpoint our location."

"Even with the cell phone?" Zoe asked.

"Possibly, but the bad guys are heading this way."

"Were they shooting at you?" Aaron asked.

"They left Pete behind to cover the area where they lost us. Just in case we found a hiding place. Smart," he murmured then shook his head. "Just as I hung up with dispatch, Pete shot at me. He's not too far away. We're going to have to come up with a plan.

If the others come back to join him, we're going to be sitting ducks."

Zoe sucked in a breath while Sophia tensed.

"Then we'll have to play a little game of hide-and-seek," Aaron said.

Lance lifted a brow. "What do you have in mind?"

"You and I are going to leave the cave and pin down where Pete is. Then I'm going to distract him while you sneak around and tackle him."

Lance grunted. "That sounds great in theory. I don't know that we should leave Zoe and Sophia in here alone."

"We'll be fine," Zoe said. "We have to do something. A plan of action is better than waiting for them to come shooting."

Lance slid his gaze to Aaron. "You have a plan to avoid getting shot while distracting him?"

Aaron nodded and removed his hat. "Oldest trick in the book. I just need a stick."

Zoe stood and stomped her feet trying to get some feeling back into them. Finally they started tingling and then hurting and she just prayed that none of them had permanent frostbite damage. But that was the least of her worries. She'd be happy with all of them getting out alive.

Aaron slipped out of the cave with Lance right behind him. Zoe positioned herself near the entrance so she could see—and help somehow if possible. Aaron wasn't a police officer, but that didn't seem to faze him as he prepared to face down a killer.

Ducking low, he searched the ground, and she saw him close his hands around a stick that suited him. Still keeping himself as small a target as possible, he placed the hat on the end of the stick then slowly raised it. Lance, hunched over and cautious, moved into the trees then stopped.

Zoe's nerves vibrated. Would it work? Would they be able to carry out such a dangerous and risky plan?

Another crack echoed through the trees and Aaron's hat flew from the stick.

Aaron hissed when his hat landed on the ground beside him. He picked up the hat in case he needed to use it again and hoped Lance was paying attention to the direction the bullet had come from. He moved a bit up the hill. As far as he could tell the bullet had come in at a downward angle. That meant the shooter was above him. He caught Lance looking at him. Aaron pointed upward.

Lance nodded and started moving. Slowly,

quietly. Where were the other men? Why hadn't they shown yet?

Then he remembered. Sophia had taken Pete's phone. He didn't have a way to contact the other two who'd gone ahead of him.

But they'd no doubt heard the shots.

Which meant he and Lance had very little time to take Pete down. Aaron moved carefully, using the trees as shields, doing his best to stay invisible. Just up ahead, he thought he saw movement. But was it Lance or Pete? Or someone else?

He stayed still, feeling his heart pound in his chest. He wasn't a hunter, but he'd grown up with three brothers and knew his way around a game of hide-and-seek in the woods. Granted, his brothers hadn't been shooting at him, but still...

More movement. Aaron lifted the hat. Nothing. He moved it to the right, away from his body. A shot sounded. The bullet whizzed by but missed the hat. Then a thud and a yell. Aaron moved faster and found Lance on top of Pete wrestling for control of Lance's weapon. Pete rolled. Lance's gun flew from his fingers, and Pete dove back into Lance and landed a solid punch on his cheek. Lance howled and struck back. Pete took the hit on his jaw, but Aaron saw him reach back to his ankle. And pull a gun from his ankle holster.

Aaron moved, kicked out. But Pete moved unexpectedly and instead of getting the man's wrist, Aaron's boot landed on Pete's forearm. Pete yelled, but didn't drop the gun, instead he turned it toward Lance and fired. Only Lance was rolling and the bullet slammed into the ground beside him. Lance rocked to his feet and went head first into Pete's gut. They both went down, Lance's hands wrapped around Pete's wrist, holding the gun away from him. Aaron couldn't get in a good kick without possibly usurping Lance's tentative advantage in the fight.

Aaron dove for Lance's weapon, got it in his hands, pulled the slide to chamber the bullet and spun to find Lance losing his grip on Pete's wrist. Pete landed a punch to Lance's midsection, and the deputy lost his hold. Pete lowered the weapon to Lance's head.

Aaron fired. Once. Twice. Center mass. Pete jerked but didn't go down. He turned the gun toward Aaron. Before he could pull the trigger, Lance knocked the gun out of his grasp. Aaron snagged it, held both guns on the bleeding, screaming man while Lance rolled him to his stomach and fastened the cuffs around his wrists.

Lance sat back on his heels and swiped at his bleeding face. He looked up at Aaron. "Thanks," he gasped.

"Yeah." He stuffed the weapon in the waistband of his jeans. "Yeah."

The sirens finally reached their ears. Aaron pulled his sweater off, leaving his long-sleeved T-shirt still on. He dropped beside Pete and pressed the material against the man's wounds. "We have to keep him alive," Aaron said.

"You work on him. I'm going to keep an eye out for the other two while I get back to the cave to check on Zoe and Sophia. I'll call Clay to tell him exactly where to come."

"Good." He glanced around. "Hopefully, these trees will be enough cover for the time being."

Aaron felt for a pulse and found it relatively strong. He must have missed anything vital. Relief flowed. As much as he hated what Pete was, he didn't want to be responsible for the man's death.

"I don't know where the other two went, but I'm guessing if they heard the sirens, they took off."

Aaron nodded. "They might be gone for now—" he looked up and caught Lance's eye "—but I don't doubt they'll be back."

FIVE

Zoe settled herself in front of the fire Aaron had finished building about thirty minutes ago. Once the authorities had arrived on the scene near the cave, things had gone quickly. They'd been ushered to the local hospital, they'd given their statements, answered a zillion questions, been examined and finally released. Sophia's sugar levels were slightly elevated, but not enough to admit her. Zoe would keep a close eye on her throughout the night.

Although it was only six o'clock in the evening, it was dark outside, the sun setting early this time of year. She stared at the dancing flames and considered the day. One day. Half a day, actually. Not even twelve hours and she felt as though she'd just lived a lifetime. She ran a hand down her cheek and decided it was probably better not to think about it. She knew things could have ended far differently, and the only thing she knew to do was be grateful it had ended the way it had—and try to figure out the *why* of it all.

Aaron came back into the den, two sodas in his hands. She looked away from the fire as he took the seat on the couch next to her. "It's over," he said.

She accepted the offered drink and popped the tab. "No, I don't think it is." She met his gaze, thinking how kind his eyes were. Deep blue and filled with an ocean of compassion, caring...and strength. To match the rest of his well-muscled physique. He really was a handsome man. She looked away and took a sip of the sugary drink. She didn't drink colas often, but tonight she wanted one while she wrestled with the fact that she was attracted to him. Which was the last thing she needed. "And neither do you." She wasn't staying in Wrangler's Corner. Being in the small town was merely a necessity right now. She would be going back to Knoxville and her life as soon as possible.

"No, I don't." He took her hand, and she let him in spite of her misgivings. "How's Sophia?"

"She's in her room cuddling with her favorite stuffed animal and watching TV, a comedy she's seen a dozen times, but never seems to tire of." She gave him a small smile. "She needs something to laugh about. Tickles, the cat, is sleeping at the foot of the bed, too."

"And she's all right staying in her room by herself?"

"For now. When it's time to go to sleep I have a feeling she'll be keeping me company." She looked back at the fire. "Have you heard from the hospital?"

"Lance called while I was in the barn with the horses. Pete survived surgery."

She squeezed his fingers. "I'm glad."

"You are?"

"Yes. It's true I'd feel safer if he was dead, but aside from living with the regret that I already see in your eyes, Pete is our only chance to find out why the men are after Sophia. But whatever happens, you shot him to save Lance, Aaron. To save us all. You're a hero as far as I'm concerned. I imagine Lance feels the same way."

He flushed and cleared his throat. "I'm no hero, Zoe."

"Maybe not in your eyes."

He took a swig of the soda then set the can on the coaster on the coffee table. Then his eyes lifted to the painting above the mantel. "That's beautiful. Who did that?"

"I did." She turned to look at the painting she'd done shortly after Sophia's seventh birthday. "It was a lovely day at the park that afternoon. So peaceful and serene. Sophia was on the swing, and I was pushing her. Trevor took the picture, and I turned it into an oil. It's one of my favorites. I couldn't leave it behind when we left Knoxville."

"Of course not."

"I was in such a hurry when we left Knoxville that I'm surprised I remembered to grab most of what I needed to continue to work."

"You're very talented. Have you been painting all your life?"

"No, just since high school. I started during a very tough time in my life. My parents were going through a pretty messy divorce and I needed an…escape. I found it in painting… and some other not so productive things." She twisted her fingers together. Now why say that? Because she wanted to confide in him? Trust him? Did her heart know something her mind didn't? He'd put his life on the line to keep her physically safe, that was true. She wasn't sure she was ready to trust him emotionally, though. And until she was, she'd better keep comments like that to herself.

"What are you going to do now?" he asked. His question surprised her. She figured he'd push for more information, more details. Moments from her past better forgotten for everyone.

She gave a slight shrug. "I don't know. I'm thankful there are deputies outside that are willing to stand guard tonight, but they can't do that every night. I guess I'll have to run again."

"Run? Again?"

She blinked. They'd been through so much over the past few hours she'd forgotten he didn't even know why she was in Wrangler's Corner. "I'm originally from Knoxville. About a month ago someone tried to kidnap Sophia while she was walking home from school."

"What?"

She nodded. "We just lived five houses down from the school. It's a pretty busy street, but she liked to walk so I let her because there was a crossing guard. The day of the incident I was standing on the front porch watching for her. The crossing guard made sure she got across the street, then when she was almost to our house, a gray sedan pulled up beside her and the back door opened. I immediately had a bad feeling and yelled at her to run. Thankfully, Sophia didn't hesitate. I guess she heard the terror in my scream. The person in the vehicle was already getting out when

Sophia took off, but he managed to grab her backpack. She slid out of it and ran as fast as she could toward me. The person drove away. I was so scared I didn't even think to get a license plate."

"What did the police say?"

"There were a lot of witnesses and confirmed it was definitely an attempted kidnapping. The police took it very seriously and looked into it. They had officers patrolling the school before and after hours for about a week and it was all over the local news, of course. But when nothing else happened, they decided whoever it was had moved on. They alerted everyone in the area to be on the lookout for the gray sedan, but truly, there are a lot of gray sedans out there. They said it was probably just a random thing and it wouldn't happen again, but I couldn't stop looking over my shoulder. I didn't want to leave Sophia with anyone, didn't want to take my eyes off her."

"I can understand that," he said softly. "So you came here?"

She hesitated. "Yes, but only after someone tried to run me off the road."

He stilled. "Run you off the road?"

"It was late at night. I'd finally been able to leave Sophia with my sister-in-law, Nina, for a few hours to go to a Bible study. On my way home, I was on one of the back roads between my house and the church. I passed a side road and headlights came on. A car pulled behind me and rammed my back end. I managed to avoid a wreck and get my car under control. The person was coming back for a second hit when several vehicles came from the opposite direction. The car drove off and I drove to Nina's house. Sophia and I just stayed there for the night. I called the police, reported it and—" She shrugged. "That's it. I'd had enough. So I emailed Amber." She gave him a flicker of a smile. "My old college roommate."

"My sister?"

"Yes."

He narrowed his eyes. "College roommate? Why don't I remember you?"

She gave him a small grin. "There's no reason you should. I came to the ranch with Amber a couple of times on weekends, but you and your brothers…well, you guys were never there much."

"And we never really paid attention to who Amber brought home."

"No, from what I recall, everyone was kind of going in their own direction. Seth was doing the rodeo thing. I remember that clearly. Clay was into law enforcement in Nashville. You were always working with an animal or away at school or something." She shrugged. "I don't really remember."

He reached out and touched her hair, let a dark curl wrap around his finger like a baby's small hand. Then he captured her gaze. "I should have paid attention." Zoe let herself get snared in his eyes for a brief moment before she cleared her throat and looked away. Aaron's hand dropped. "So, you ran. And now this. You're being targeted."

She nodded. "It looks that way."

"But why?"

She shook her head and looked up at him again. "I truly don't know. I make a decent living with my painting and I have some money from my husband's life insurance policy, but it's not enough to commit a crime for."

"You'd be surprised," he murmured. "What happened to your husband?"

"He was killed in a car wreck." She swallowed and looked away. "Just about a year ago."

"I'm sorry."

Tears threatened. "I am, too. He was a good man." And he'd deserved better than her. But she'd keep that to herself.

"I'm sure he was."

"Regardless," she said, "I don't know why anyone would be after Sophia. I mean I can think of what some people would do with a kidnapped child and it makes me sick to my stomach, but truly, for someone to go to this much trouble to get her…" She bit her lip and shook her head as she looked down at her hands. "I mean, sure, I can see someone spotting a child walking home alone and thinking it's a good opportunity to snatch her. But when that plan was thwarted, wouldn't you think he'd move on to someone else? Why keep coming back for her? Why go to all this trouble? Something else is going on, but I just don't know what it is—or how to go about finding out what it might be."

"You have a good point. And one other thing."

"What?"

"You said that the back door opened. That means there was more than one person involved in the attempted snatch."

"Yes. The police mentioned that, as well," she said. "And, no, I can't think of anyone who would do something like that. Believe me, I've thought about it. At first, though, I figured it was just a random act. You know, someone who was cruising the school zone, watching for a child walking alone or something. They saw Sophia and didn't realize I was looking for her."

"But?"

"But then I realized after someone went after me that it wasn't random. Someone was targeting us. And that terrifies me not just because I'm afraid they're going to try again, but because I don't know how to prepare for it, defend against it—or from which direction the next attack will come."

"Hey." He placed a finger under her chin and lifted it until their eyes met. "You have help now. You're not alone in this. We'll figure it out."

She felt the heat rise in her cheeks. "We?"

"Yes. We. And Clay and Lance." He smiled. "What's the point in having cop friends and family if they can't help you out once in a while? Although, I will say Lance and the others might actually be more help than Clay right now. He's a bit distracted with his wife due to have their baby any day now."

Her lower lip trembled. She hadn't felt quite so…what? Cared for? Protected? Yes, to both. She hadn't felt either in over a year. Maybe even longer. It felt strange…and wonderful all at the same time. She sighed. "Well, I hope they can find the men who did this so they can't hurt anyone else." Or come back to try again.

"You and me both." He rubbed his chin and studied her. "So tell me more about yourself. Your background. I know you were married, but your husband died in a car wreck." He glanced at the oil painting again. "I know you're incredibly talented. And I also know you have a daughter who's smart as a whip. And I know you're both in danger."

She pulled in a deep breath and let it out slowly. "Yes, that about sums it up."

A low chuckle rumbled in his chest. "I don't believe it. There's got to be more."

There was more all right. She mentally flipped through the things she could tell him that wouldn't send him flying out the door. "I have a good church in Knoxville and some good friends that I've left behind. I love my job. Being able to work from home, painting portraits, that's my dream come true. It's a great job for a single mom." She gave a soft laugh. "Painting is also my therapy. I really enjoy the people, the clients, that I get to work with."

"What about Sophia?"

"Sophia has a few friends from school, but she's not the most social kid. She and I spend a lot of time together and I like that.

Our next-door neighbor has a girl about Sophia's age and they run back and forth between the houses, but Sophia is happy on the farm with the animals and never wants to leave."

"What about you? Are you happy on the farm?"

"Yes. I grew up on one. Even though my father worked as an accountant, he inherited the land that we lived on. I think he was considering selling but then…everything kind of blew up and my parents divorced." She shrugged. "That's about it."

He reached out and ran a finger down her cheek. "All surface information. I want to know *you*."

Zoe stiffened. "What do you want to know?"

"Why did you turn to my sister for help? Why not go home to your parents? Are they still living?"

"They're alive."

"But?"

"We're not close." His eyes narrowed and she wanted to squirm, but refused. "I had a rather rocky upbringing. Like I said, my parents split up. They divorced when I was in high school. They each went their own way and aren't interested in pretending to be a family when the holidays roll around. So we just do our own thing. I send them a card with Sophia's picture each Christmas and call it good."

"That's really sad."

She shrugged. "Yes, it is, but it's okay, too. I've accepted it and moved on. I don't let it bother me." Much. Holidays were definitely worse than other times during the year, though.

He shook his head. "Do you have any brothers and sisters?"

"A brother. He's older than I am and was headed to college when my parents divorced."

"And you two don't talk?"

She hesitated then slowly shook her head. "I don't even know where he is."

She could tell she'd shocked him. A man who was so tight with his family wouldn't be able to comprehend her dysfunctional background.

"Why don't you know where he is?"

She shook her head. How could she explain the horrendous fight she and Toby had had before he'd left. That her last words to him had been *I hate you. Get out. I never want to see you again.* How did she explain the year she'd spent in rehab, getting her life straightened out, getting her heart right with the God she'd thought had surely given up on her? How did she tell him that she was not only in physical danger, she was in the middle of a faith crisis, as well? "We had words. An argument about him going to college and leaving me to deal with the fallout of our parents' marriage. I know he didn't leave me because he wanted to. He had to go. He wasn't strong, either, and couldn't handle staying at home. He would often get in between my parents, trying to be a buffer and it wore on him. Emotionally, physically." She shook her head. "So, he left, and we lost touch for a while and by the time I was in a position to reach out to him, I didn't know where to reach out *to.*" She'd searched for him, though. She'd tried to find him at college only to learn he'd dropped out. She'd checked all of his friends she could think of and no one had seen him. She'd even reported him missing to the police and they'd turned up nothing. Her heart had broken and she'd just assumed he might have changed his name to get away from the reporters and their constant questions about their father's criminal activities. "I don't know why they went after him like they did. Maybe because no one ever expected it." She certainly hadn't believe it. She shrugged. "I really don't know."

Aaron wanted to ask more questions. She could see them in his eyes, rolling onto the tip of his tongue, and weariness swept over her. She didn't want to answer any more questions. Not now. She stood. "I'm just going to check on Sophia."

He nodded. "Sure."

She went to Sophia's room, her mind spinning, emotions scattered. She had to get herself together. Talking about her past had shaken her. She didn't need to reveal any more of herself to this man. She was leaving. She had to take Sophia and they had to run. There was no sense in pouring her heart out to Aaron in her den. No point in getting to know him or letting him get to know her. Being vulnerable didn't sit well with her. She wasn't comfortable with it.

She walked into Sophia's room and found her daughter asleep, arms wrapped around her favorite stuffed animal. She looked so peaceful Zoe didn't bother her. She just backed out and shut the door leaving it cracked so she could hear if Sophia called out to her.

For a moment she simply stood in the hallway and pressed her forehead to the doorjamb. *Lord, please show me how to protect my child, help me to be wise in the choices I make and the people I trust.*

Because she knew that if she didn't have

some divine intervention, things were not going to end well for her or Sophia.

Aaron fielded the numerous texts from his family members while he waited for Zoe to return. With sadness in his heart, he realized she'd texted and called no one to tell about her ordeal. His family might drive him crazy sometimes, but at least they were there. It was a huge comfort to know he could count on them and that they loved him unconditionally. Just like they all loved his sister, Amber, and were glad to see her when she put in an appearance, but didn't expect her to be around much.

He couldn't imagine being so terribly alone in the world. And he wanted to help Zoe, he really did.

He'd meant it when he said that she had help, that he and Clay and Lance would work with her to figure out who was behind the attack here at the ranch, but he needed to put the brakes on his attraction for her. No, more than that, he needed to bury it. Deep. He'd picked up on her reticence to share about herself with him and he couldn't help but wonder why. She was hiding something, but what? He rubbed his eyes. It didn't matter. Falling for the single mom would be a huge mistake. Hadn't he already learned that lesson?

She stepped back into the den and took her seat on the couch. She'd changed into sweats and a long-sleeved T-shirt. Her sleeves hung midpalm, and she looked comfortable. And vulnerable. And incredibly attractive. "Sophia fell asleep," she murmured.

"She's had a long day."

"Mmm. Yes. A traumatic one. I pray she doesn't have nightmares."

"Or you, either. Are you going to be able to sleep?" he asked.

"I don't know. I might doze, but I'll probably sit in the recliner with Mr. Updike's .45 Winchester."

"You know how to use it?"

"I wouldn't touch it if I didn't." Her eyes flashed. "And I won't be caught without a weapon again."

He lifted a brow, and a deep respect started to build. She might need help, but she'd do her best to help herself, as well. Looking at her now, he couldn't imagine he'd thought her fragile or helpless. The vulnerability had disappeared with the lift of her chin and now he thought she looked strong and capable. As well as intensely determined. "Good," he said and stood. "I guess I'll head on home." He spotted a pad and pen by the recliner and snagged the items. He wrote on the top sheet of the pad. "Here's my cell number and my parents' landline number. And here's Clay's personal cell number." He set the pad back on the table. "If you need anything at all, just call and someone will be here before you can hang up, all right?"

He saw her blink back tears. She nodded. "Okay," she whispered. "Thanks."

"You're welcome, Zoe." He grabbed his coat. Once he had his gloves on, he looked back at her and swallowed. Her eyes beckoned. He could see the fear still lingering. "You'll be safe tonight."

"Yes, tonight."

He backed toward the door. He had to get out of there before he did something stupid like take her in his arms and hug her. Or kiss her. He nearly tripped, righted himself and closed his hand around the door knob. He cleared his throat. "I'm just going to check on the heifer and the calf, and then I'll be on my way."

"Of course. Thank you again for everything, Aaron. I know how much I owe you."

"You don't owe me a thing. Get some rest." He forced his gaze away from the shimmer of her dark eyes. With supreme effort, he opened the door and walked out.

The sharp wind hit him full in the face and he shivered. He might be used to the bitter cold, but that didn't mean he liked it. Picturing himself on a tropical beach, playing in the sand with Sophia or swimming in the surf with Zoe, he pulled his scarf from his pocket and wrapped it so that the cold didn't cut as bad. Then he blinked the images from his head. If he was going to bury his attraction for Zoe, he couldn't be imagining beach days with her. He looked around. But if they did wind up somewhere, it would definitely be a beach. No skiing. He was ready for warm weather. But not with Zoe. No way. That kind of thinking would only lead to heartache.

The snow had stopped for now, but the way the air smelled said there was more to come.

He spotted the Wrangler's Corner police cruisers. One was positioned strategically near the barn with a view of the back of the house and one right out front. He squinted and waved. Ronnie Hart, who had a good view of the back of the building, waved back. A new deputy who'd been hired about a month ago, Ginny Garrison, also lifted a hand in acknowledgement then typed something into the computer she had open on the tray attached to the dash.

Probably making note of his departure. He walked over to Ronnie, and the man lowered his window. "Thanks for watching out for her."

"No problem. Nice job out there on the mountain."

He still couldn't believe he'd shot the man. Pete. The man had a name. "I couldn't let him shoot Lance."

"For sure. Maybe you should hang up your stethoscope and go to the police academy."

Aaron laughed but it had little humor. "No way. I'm happy being a vet." He nodded in the direction of the barn. "I'm just going to check on Lily and then I'm heading home." He glanced back at the house and saw the flickering of the television through the curtains. So sleep wouldn't come any time soon for her. He wondered if she would actually be able to doze off.

"You think those guys will be back?"

Aaron looked back at Ronnie. "Yes. Unfortunately, I do."

Ronnie nodded and patted his weapon. "Then we'll be ready."

Aaron's jaw tightened and he felt for the weapon he'd retrieved from the kitchen table where it had been left when everyone scattered from the house earlier. The weight of it against his side brought comfort, reassurance. "Yes. Yes, we will."

SIX

Zoe couldn't bring herself to sleep in her room. Instead she'd lain down beside Sophia and figured she'd spare the child waking in the middle of the night to come find her. Careful not to disturb the still-sleeping Sophia, she rolled over to check the clock.

Seven forty-five.

So she'd actually slept. She really hadn't thought she would, but having the two deputies outside had allowed her adrenaline to settle down. She slid out from underneath the covers. Goose bumps pebbled her skin, and she shivered. She needed to bump the heat up a notch.

On sock-covered feet, she padded to the window and pushed the curtain aside to peer out. She could see Lance sitting in the cruiser sipping coffee from a thermos cup. A light dusting of snow covered the car. Ronnie must have left and Lance had taken over sometime during the night. He glanced up, saw her looking and lifted a hand. She waved back, then released the curtain and let it fall back into place. She walked to the thermostat, knocked the heat up two degrees then hurried to her room at the opposite end of the hall.

After a quick shower, she went to her room and pulled on warm clothes, a hat and her boots. As she dressed, she thought about her situation. How had she gotten to this point? Whom had she made so mad that he or she wanted to kill her? It made no sense and only made her brain hurt to think about so she switched gears to breakfast. She mentally ran down the list of the items in her refrigerator and decided she had enough food for everyone. The least she could do was feed the two deputies who'd spent the majority of their night watching over her house. But the animals came first. When she stepped outside, Lance opened the door to his cruiser to join her. "Everything all right?"

She shot him a smile and let her gaze roam the area. "Yes, as of right now, everything is fine. I just have to take care of the animals."

As they were speaking, Aaron's SUV pulled into the drive. Her heart flipped and she had no choice but to acknowledge that she was glad to see him this morning. He parked next to Lance, climbed out and shut the door. When he turned, his blue eyes landed on her and flashed with pleasure. "Morning, y'all."

So. He was as glad to see her as she was him. Butterflies swarmed and she crossed her arms even as she nodded. "Morning." She couldn't fall for him. She couldn't. He was a good man. A good man who deserved a good woman. A woman who didn't bring danger and heartbreak with her. She cleared her throat.

"I haven't heard otherwise so I'm guessing you had a quiet night?" he said.

He'd been worried. "It was quiet, thanks. I'm just headed to the barn to take care of the animals. If you'll give me about thirty minutes, I'll fix you all breakfast."

Lance's brow rose. "Sounds good to me. If Aaron and I help you, you'll finish faster."

She smiled. "Hungry?"

"Starved. I'll do just about anything legal for a home-cooked meal. Just ask Mrs. Starke."

Zoe laughed. "Come on then. We can knock this out in no time."

The three worked together in the barn caring for the animals. She let the horses out into the pasture, filled the barn cats' bowls with water and food and made sure most of the stalls were clean for the horses' return. There were two horses who needed a little extra attention, but she had hungry men on her hands so she'd do the other two later. They could wait an hour or so.

Aaron checked on the calf and the new mother. The little one nudged up against his mother looking for his breakfast. Zoe watched them and smiled. "I love animals. They have so few expectations, want so little. Food, water and a warm place to sleep."

He looked up. "We should all be that way, huh?"

She shrugged. "Maybe. Right now, all I want is my child to be safe and I want to stay alive so I can take care of her."

"We're going to make that happen."

She blinked against the sudden surge of tears and drew in a deep breath. She needed a change of subject. "Sophia's excited to come out and see the calf. They seem to be doing well."

"They're doing great," he said. "When it warms up a bit, we'll let them out in the pasture with the others."

Aaron ran a gloved hand down the calf's back, his touch gentle and caring. She wondered what it would be like to be on the receiving end of that tenderness.

Actually, she already knew the answer to

that question. Hadn't he held her in the cave when she'd been afraid? Hadn't he treated Sophia with the utmost gentleness and caring when she'd been so afraid?

Zoe rubbed her head where the beginning of a headache threatened. What was she thinking? She needed to focus on keeping Sophia safe and figuring out who was after her, not daydreaming about romance with a man. And this man in particular. She looked up and his gaze snagged hers. "Thank you, Aaron. For everything." She knew she sounded like a broken record with her thanks, but she wanted to make sure he understood how much she appreciated him and his efforts.

His eyes softened further. "You're welcome." His gloved hand ensnared hers, and he gave it a little squeeze. Her heart thudded a little faster, and she returned the squeeze even as her brain sent warning signals about getting too close to him. "Come on, I'm starving," he said.

"Me, too. Let's get cleaned up and we'll eat."

She stood at the kitchen sink, letting the water warm up as she tried to steer her thoughts from the fact that the good-looking vet had stolen his way into her heart in such a short period of time. She sighed and finished washing up then let the men do the same while she got started on breakfast. Twenty minutes later she had bacon, eggs and pancakes on platters. Pitchers of orange juice sat on the table and the coffee finished dripping into the carafe. She pulled the plates down and set the table. Then she hauled down enough glasses and placed them next to the plates.

Aaron entered the kitchen and lifted his nose, testing the air. "Something sure smells good."

"There's plenty, too. Could you get that bottle of syrup from the pantry for me?"

"Sure." He crossed to the room and opened the pantry door. She moved to grab the salt and pepper from beside the stove, and they both turned at the same time. Her nose bumped his hard bicep, and she lost her balance. His free arm came around her waist and kept her from bouncing back into the stove. "You okay?"

His musky scent wafted over her. The strength of his arms gave her security. His nearness made her yearn for things she'd been trying to put from her mind. And now it was all back and she had to ignore it all again. She swallowed. "I'm fine." He let her go. Reluctantly, she thought. "Let's dig in." She moved away from Aaron and stepped to the window to wave to Ginny who still sat in the cruiser watching the area.

Ginny came inside, and Zoe started moving the platters of food to the table. She was reaching for the pitcher of orange juice when Aaron's hand brushed hers. She froze for a slight second and let the sensation wash through her. When she looked up, he gave her a faint smile. "I'll get it."

She gave a little nod. He'd done that on purpose. He knew he unsettled her and was having a little fun with it. She couldn't say she minded. "Okay. Thank you."

Sophia came into the kitchen rubbing her eyes and yawning. She stopped mid-yawn when she saw everyone at the table. Zoe walked over and smoothed her child's bed hair. "We've got company."

Sophia shrugged. "Hi."

Aaron slid out of the chair beside him. "Wanna sit with me?"

"Sure." Sophia climbed into the chair next to him and studied him. "How's the baby calf?"

"She's doing just fine. Her mama is taking good care of her."

Sophia scratched her nose and looked at Zoe. "Just like my mama takes care of me."

"Exactly."

"And you do, too."

"I do?"

"Yes. You protected us from the men shooting at us so I think that qualifies as taking care of us." Zoe choked on a laugh and turned away to hide her grin. Then she heard Sophia again. "Did you stay outside of my house all night?" She shifted her gaze slightly and saw that Sophia was talking to Ginny and Lance.

"All night," Ginny said as she dumped a helping of eggs onto her plate. She licked her lips. "And it was worth it. I'd take this in place of my regular paycheck any day."

"I'll be sure to pass that on to Clay," Lance said.

Ginny snickered. "I'll deny it."

Lance grinned. "Too late. I've got witnesses. Right, Sophia?"

Sophia's gaze darted back and forth between the two. "I'll take the fifth."

Lance, Ginny and Aaron cracked up and Aaron tweaked Sophia's nose. "Where did you hear that?"

"My daddy said it one time when mama asked him if he liked the new dish she'd fixed for dinner one night."

"Smart man," Lance murmured.

"He'd have been smarter if he'd just said he liked it if you ask me." More laughter, and Sophia beamed at being the center of attention.

Zoe heard their banter and even smiled at Sophia's precociousness. But she couldn't help the shudder that ripped through her at the memory of why the deputies were needed at her home. It was all well and good to be friends with them, but friendship wasn't why they were here.

Zoe sat at the table and stared at the people who surrounded her. Good people. People who didn't even really know her, but had fought to keep her and Sophia safe. A lump of gratitude wanted to form in her throat, but she forced it back and took a bite of the eggs.

"Mmm, this is amazing," Ginny said. "My sister would love this."

"Who's your sister?" Sophia asked.

"Her name is Tracy."

"Where is she?"

Sadness flickered in Ginny's eyes, making Zoe curious. Ginny finally said, "She's at a special home in Nashville."

"What kind of special home?" Sophia asked.

"It's for people who have special needs."

"Like what?" Sophia asked.

"Honey—" Zoe tried to stop the line of questioning, but Ginny shook her head.

"It's okay. I don't get a chance to talk about her much. Tracy is mentally disabled, which just means her brain works in different ways than yours and mine."

"I know what you mean." Sophia nodded. "There's a boy like that in my class. My teacher says he's special needs. His name is Todd and he's got Down Syndrome plus he stutters. But I like him cuz he's nice and he picked up my paper for me when Jordan pushed it off my desk." Sophia stabbed her eggs. "I like Todd a lot better than Jordan."

Ginny's eyes softened. "Then you understand. Tracy's a great girl. You'd like her."

"How old is she?"

"She's twenty. She'll be twenty-one next month."

"Maybe you can take me to meet her some day. We can take her some of my mom's cooking. She'd probably like that."

Ginny let out a small laugh. "You're right about that."

Sophia turned her attention back to her food, and Ginny continued to express her pleasure at the breakfast treat.

But Zoe couldn't seem to relax and enjoy the food. In fact, if she were eating sawdust she might not recognize the difference. Indecision and uncertainty swarmed within her. What should she do now? She looked up and found Aaron watching her.

He gave her a small frown. "You okay?"

She nodded but couldn't answer. She looked away then back up. Glanced between him and Lance and Ginny. "So what happens now? I mean you can't stay outside my house all night every night. What are my options?"

Lance put his fork down and wiped his mouth with the napkin. "Clay's asked me to head the investigation. His wife is due any day now so he's sticking close to home. We need to look at your background, any enemies you might have formed. Is there anyone who'd come looking for revenge for any reason?"

Zoe swallowed hard. Her background. How she didn't want to have to go there. "I had a few pretty wild teenage years," she said softly, "but nothing that would send someone after me after all this time. I haven't been in touch with anyone from high school in years."

"What about college?"

She shrugged and shook her head. "No, by the time I got to college, I'd cleaned up my act and had my head on straight. My parents' divorce was ugly. I was messed up and confused about a lot of things. And then I met Nan Livingston. She saw something in me that she decided was worth investing in. Because of her, I was able to dream, develop goals and plans and I knew that if I wanted to achieve those then I had to focus. So I did." That was the simple version, but all truth. Thinking about Nan brought a pang of grief, sharp and fast. It pained Zoe to think of what Nan would say about her current spiritual state.

"What about your husband?" Aaron asked. "He was killed in a wreck a year ago, right?"

"Yes."

"Was he involved in anything that he shouldn't have been a part of?"

She was shaking her head before he finished the question. "No way. Trevor was as straight as they come. A rule follower to the nth degree. There was only black and white for him, and he never deviated from doing the right thing." She knew now that was why she'd been so drawn to him. She'd craved the stability she saw in him. "I met him in college, and we hit it right off. We got married six months after we met and then had Sophia. He was a good man." She looked at Sophia who was listening with wide eyes. "And a great dad."

"I miss him," Sophia said with a sigh. "I miss going with him and Grandpop to see Thunderbolt race."

"I know, baby."

"Thunderbolt?" Aaron asked.

"Our horse," Zoe said. "Or rather, Trevor's. He enjoyed owning a racehorse. Trevor and Alexander, Trevor's father, would take Sophia to the racetrack to cheer on Thunderbolt. It was something they all did together." She smiled. "There was no gambling involved, Trevor didn't believe in it. But he loved to watch the horses race."

"Grandpop told Daddy he should sell Thunderbolt and get his money while he had a winner, but I'm glad he didn't."

"I am, too." Zoe ran a finger down her little girl's cheek. "Trevor took a lot of pleasure in that horse. The fact that he got to spend time with his father and Sophia doing something he loved just made it that much sweeter." She gave a little shrug. "So, no. This has nothing to do with Trevor. I don't know *what* it has to do with, but it's not him."

Aaron couldn't help but wonder if she was right. She sounded so positive, but could Trevor have been involved in something without Zoe knowing about it? Probably. Most spouses could manage to hide things from the other one if they truly wanted to. But had Trevor been one of those? That was the question.

Aaron downed the last of his coffee then set the cup in front of him. He looked at Lance. "So, until we figure out what all of this is about, what's the plan to keep Zoe and Sophia safe?"

Lance sipped his orange juice and shook his head. "I'll talk to Clay, and we'll come up with something. I definitely don't think they should be alone."

A knock on the door sounded, and Aaron saw Zoe jump. She settled a hand over her heart, took a deep breath and started to rise. Aaron placed a hand on her arm. "I'll get it."

He pulled his weapon, and Lance stood, too. "If it was one of the bad guys from yesterday, I don't think he'd be knocking," Lance said.

"I know, but I'm just being careful."

Lance and Ginny both pulled their guns and held them ready. "Good idea, but while there are cops in the house, let us handle it. Put your gun away."

Aaron did so and Lance walked to the door, staying to the side and not moving in front of the windows. He peered out and relaxed, shoving his weapon back in his holster. "It's Clay." He opened the door.

Clay stepped inside and nodded. "Morning."

"Morning," Aaron said. "What brings you out here this early?"

"I'd thought I'd drop in and check on Zoe and Sophia, but I'm glad you're here."

"You need something to do while waiting for that baby to be born?"

Clay scowled at him and Aaron couldn't help the small smile that lifted his lips. Clay was always the one in control. "You find me amusing right now, don't you?"

"A bit."

"Thanks."

"Anytime."

Clay's features morphed into concern. "I wanted to let you know that there won't be any charges brought against you on the shooting yesterday."

Aaron let out a slow breath. "Thanks. I wasn't really worried, but you never know."

"Yeah, well, with all the testimony from Lance and Zoe as to what happened, it's an open-and-shut deal."

"How is he?" Aaron asked. "The man I shot."

"He's still alive, but unconscious. I've got

a deputy on him and orders to be notified as soon as he wakes up so I can question him."

"Do you know who he is?" Zoe asked.

"Peter Garrett. A guy with a rap sheet as long as your arm. Robbery, assault—"

"Murder?" Aaron asked.

"No, everything but that."

"Well, he was willing to add it to the list yesterday," Lance muttered.

"Yeah. Fortunately, he failed. We did manage to take into custody a man by the name of Cody Jansen."

"Blond hair, blue eyes and mean as a snake?" Aaron asked.

"Sounds like one and the same." Clay tapped the screen of his phone and brought up the mug shot. He turned it around so Aaron could see. Zoe moved closer to look over his shoulder. She gave a small gasp. "That's him."

"Yep," Aaron agreed.

"He's got a bullet in his shoulder. He showed up in a Knoxville hospital, and officers there nabbed him. He's under arrest, but so far is refusing to talk." Clay rubbed his eyes, and Aaron thought he looked tired.

"I might have shot him, too." He blinked as he remembered pulling the trigger as the man came through the small hallway. "There was so much chaos, bullets were flying and all I could think of was to make sure I got Zoe and Sophia out of there before one of *them* got shot."

Clay clapped him on the back. "Not to worry. We'll get it all figured out. You won't be held responsible for defending yourself and them, but when all this goes to court, you'll have to testify."

"I'm ready."

"I figured you would be. I've already got your gun from yesterday so we'll have ballistics run tests to see what bullets came from what gun. I hope to return the weapon to you before too long."

Aaron nodded. "It's fine. I have another one at home I can carry until then. How's Sabrina?" Aaron asked.

Clay swallowed. "She's fine. Just fine. Really good. Yeah. She's...fine."

"Okay," Aaron said with a raised brow, "maybe that was the wrong question. How are *you*?"

Clay scowled at him. "I'm fine, too. Or I will be as soon as the baby gets here." He huffed out a breath and shook his head. "Can't stand all this waiting."

Aaron clapped him on the shoulder. "Well, that's no surprise, you've never been good at being patient. Hang in there, big brother."

"Yeah." Clay settled his Stetson back on his head. "All right, I'm out of here then. Ginny, you want to head on over to the hospital to relieve Ronnie? I'm sure he's ready to get home."

"Sure thing, Sheriff." She finished off her last bite of eggs, grabbed her coat and gloves. "Thanks for the breakfast," she said to Zoe. "It was delicious. Wish I could cook like that."

Zoe smiled. "You're welcome. And anytime you want to learn, I'm happy to give you a few lessons."

Ginny grinned. "I might just take you up on that. Tracy would flip." She slipped out the door and Aaron heard her cruiser engine come to life. He looked at Zoe. Cooking lessons? Did that mean she planned on sticking around for a while? The smile slipped from her lips, and her eyes shadowed. Was she wondering the same thing?

Clay started to leave then turned back to her. "Who did you tell that you were leaving Knoxville and coming to Wrangler's Corner?"

"No one. The day after someone tried to run me off the road, I went home from Nina's, packed my car with what I thought we'd need, and left."

"Did you notice anyone following you?"

"No. And I was looking. I drove around for hours before finding an out-of-the-way hotel. We stayed there for about a week before Amber got back to me with this ranch-sitting opportunity."

Clay blinked. "Amber got you this job?"

Aaron explained what she'd told him last night. Clay shook his head. "Glad to know she's talking to someone," he muttered.

Aaron understood. Their sister's job as a travel writer took her all over the world, and she rarely made it home—or answered her phone. Email was definitely the best way to reach her. "All right, well, stay put and—"

Zoe's gasp cut him off.

Aaron frowned. "What is it?"

"Smoke, I think." She moved closer to the window, and her eyes widened. "The barn. It's on fire!"

Zoe grabbed her coat and headed for the door then looked back at Sophia. The child's eyes were wide and filled with fear. She couldn't leave Sophia alone. Clay went to the window, peered out then came back. "I'll stay here. If this is some ploy to get us out of the house and leave you alone with her, we're not going to let that happen." He looked at Lance.

"You and Aaron go. Zoe, you stay here with me and Sophia."

She shook her head. "I can't do that. This is my responsibility. My fault. You stay here with her," she beseeched him, torn between the desire to stay with her child and keep her promise to take care of the place. But Clay was a police officer. She had full confidence in his ability to protect Sophia. Much better than she could for sure. "Keep her safe, Clay, you hear me? Keep her safe."

Zoe raced out the door with Aaron on her heels, and Clay's frustrated shout ringing in her ears. Lance brought up the rear, but he didn't bother to argue with her. There was no time to consider how foolishly she might be behaving. As long as Sophia was safe, Zoe's only thought was to take care of the property she'd been entrusted with.

Smoke now poured from the open door. She covered her nose and mouth with her scarf and stepped inside. The two horses she'd left in their stalls whinnied their fear and paced restlessly in the confined space. The thick smoke nearly blinded her, and Zoe squinted against the haze. "Where's the fire?" she asked. Then coughed.

Aaron stepped in behind her and pulled the collar of his coat up over his mouth and nose.

Through the haze, she could see him, but visibility was getting worse by the second. He pointed. "There!"

At the end of the barn, she could make out flashes of orange. "The hay," she said. "You let the animals out. I'll get the extinguishers. There are two in the office."

"Be careful!" Aaron hollered at her even as he moved to the stalls of the two horses. Aaron released them and they headed for the exit without hesitation. Zoe entered the office and grabbed the first extinguisher from its mount on the wall then snagged the one behind the desk. She raced back into the center of the barn to see Aaron leading the mama heifer and her baby out. When she came up behind him, he held out a hand and she slapped the larger extinguisher in it. Lance had already pulled the hose from the rack and cranked the water on full blast. He began to drag it toward the back of the barn wetting everything in his path.

Once the animals were safely out, she and Aaron moved through the smoke. The heat was intense, the flames already reaching for the nearest wooden stall. She pulled the pin and held the held the nozzle of the extinguisher toward the flames.

Aaron came up beside her and did the

same. At first the flames fought back and Zoe despaired that the extinguishers weren't doing any good. She struggled for breath and began to grow dizzy, but gritted her teeth and held the stream of foam steady. And slowly, they started to win the battle. The flames flickered then faded. But the smoke was fierce.

She dropped the extinguisher and went to her knees, her lungs straining and finally succumbing to the lack of oxygen.

A hand on her upper arm pulled her to her feet, and she stumbled after Aaron. Lance held on to her other arm and the three of them exited the barn into the fresh air. "Are you okay?" Aaron gasped then gave a hacking cough.

Zoe sank to the cold ground and gasped, sucked in the fresh air, coughed and finally felt the world settle. "Yes. I think so. Are you?"

He nodded. "Lance?"

"Yeah."

A sharp crack broke the air, and Zoe felt a burning sting along her left arm.

"Get behind the tractor," Lance yelled. "Someone's shooting!"

SEVEN

Just as in the barn, Aaron grabbed her right arm and headed toward the tractor. Lance had his weapon out and was right beside him, his back toward Aaron, his gun aimed in the direction the shot had come from. Aaron pulled her around the front of the tractor and she slumped to the ground, her back against the heavy rubber tire. Lance rounded to the other tire and hovered there.

Aaron's heart thumped hard in his chest and he dropped to his knees in front of Zoe. "I'm getting really tired of being shot at."

"Tell me about it," Zoe muttered. She shifted and sucked in a deep breath. "Ow."

He looked down and saw blood seeping through her heavy tan coat. Fear thrummed through him. "Oh, no, Zoe, you're hit." He scooted closer.

"Hit?" She frowned. "As in shot?" She didn't protest as he slid her wounded arm out of the sleeve. She gave a low hiss of pain but otherwise stayed silent.

"Yes, but the fact that you're talking and making sense is encouraging." He looked up at Lance. "You see the shooter?"

"Not yet."

"Lance? Aaron?" Clay shouted.

Aaron turned and peered around Zoe and the tire. "We're okay, Clay! Zoe's hit, though not bad."

"You're sure she's okay?"

Aaron examined the wound. No bullet hole, but a nice groove in her upper arm that would need a few stitches. "I'm sure."

"Backup's on the way. Stay put. I've got Sophia right here with me and she's fine."

Zoe seemed to deflate once she heard that Sophia was safe. Her eyes closed, and she leaned her head back against the tire. Another shot rang out. A puff of white snow lifted into the air just next to the tractor. Aaron flinched and tucked his head against his chest. Zoe drew in a deep breath, but didn't move. Prayers slipped from his lips.

This time the sound of gunfire came from the house. Zoe shot into a sitting position. "Sophia!" Aaron spun to see Clay at the window shooting back into the direction the original shot came from.

"It's okay, she's all right. It's just Clay. He must have seen something." And been absolutely sure of what he was shooting at or he wouldn't have fired back. Sirens wailed in the distance, and Aaron let out a slow breath, hoping the sound would scare the shooter off the property. And that someone would be able to chase him down and catch him.

Police cruisers pulled into the drive and parked in front of the house. The car doors opened, and officers stayed behind the protection they offered. "Who went to the woods? The shots came from the woods behind the barn." Clay's voice came from behind the cracked front door.

"Parker and Joy." Aaron thought he recognized Walter Haywood's voice in response to Clay's question. Parker Little and Joy West were two other deputies with the rapidly expanding Wrangler's Corner sheriff's department.

"Stay put until we hear from them," Clay ordered. "Aaron, Lance? You still okay?"

"We're all right," Lance called back. He caught Aaron's gaze. "How bad is it?"

"Not that bad." Zoe's pale features worried him. Her eyes were open and watching, though. He leaned in for a closer look. "A couple of stitches, and you'll be fine. Okay?"

"Yes, it stings, but I don't think I'm going to die from it."

If he thought there was any chance she was in danger of dying from the wound, they wouldn't still be behind the tire. Somehow they'd be on the way to the hospital. He shrugged out of his jacket and pulled his sweater and long-sleeved T-shirt over his head. He yanked the sweater back on then fished in his jeans for the pocketknife he'd started carrying.

If he was ever duct-taped again, at least he'd have a fighting chance. Using the knife, he cut off one of the sleeves and wrapped it around her upper arm, pulling it tight to stop the bleeding and to hold the edges of the wound together. He looked at her. "Best I can do without my medical kit."

"It's fine," she whispered. "Thanks."

"It needs to be washed out and you probably need a round of antibiotics, but we'll have to worry about that a little later." She gave him a tight, grim smile and shifted with a grimace. "Pain pills might not be a bad idea, either."

"No," she bit out, her eyes hard, jaw tight. "No pills."

Aaron raised a brow. "Okay. No one's going

to force them down your throat." He pulled her coat back around her, leaving her arm free of the sleeve, but under the warm material.

She sighed. "Sorry. Didn't mean to snap. I...I used to have a drug problem."

He froze for a slight second as her words registered. He saw her face flame red and knew she was already regretting her words. "It's all right," he said. "No pain pills then." He looked at Lance. "Haven't heard any shots for a few minutes."

"Yeah." He glanced toward the house. "Clay hasn't said to move yet."

Several tense minutes passed and Aaron thought his heart might beat out of his chest thanks to his rushing adrenaline. Movement near the tree line captured his attention. "Lance?"

"I see it."

"Hold your fire," Clay called out. "Joy's near the trees. The shooter's gone."

Lance stood. Aaron waited a few seconds then helped Zoe to her feet. She held her arm against her stomach and he kept a steadying hand at her back. "Let's get inside and get that cleaned up."

Aaron led her to the house while Clay and his deputies discussed strategy. Clay had already notified the proper authorities of the incident with a request to have neighboring law enforcement available should they be needed until the shooter was caught.

"Sophia?" Zoe called. "Where are you?"

"Mom!" Sophia rushed from the den to her mother.

Zoe wrapped her good arm around her child and held on tight. "It's okay, baby. It's okay."

"Sheriff Starke pulled the couch from the wall and told me to get behind it. He told me to stay right there between the couch and the wall and I did."

Zoe kissed the top of Sophia's head. "I'm very proud of you for obeying." Her eyes filled, and she looked at Clay. "Thank you for keeping her safe."

"Of course," Clay said.

Sophia pulled back and frowned at the blood on her mother's arm. "Why are you bleeding? Are you hurt? What's wrong?"

Sophia shrugged the rest of the way out of the jacket and Aaron took it form her. "I'm okay," she said. "It's just a scratch."

He watched them together and felt his heart clench. They were all each other had at this point. "What happens to Sophia if something happens to you?" he asked her quietly.

She stilled. "She goes to live with Trevor's sister, Nina, and her husband, Gregory."

"And does Sophia come with any money attached?"

Zoe swallowed and he saw her follow his line of thinking. "Um. Sophia," she said, "will you go get the first-aid kit out of the bathroom?"

Sophia pressed her lips into a tight line and didn't release her grip on her mother. She looked back and forth between the adults then nodded. "Sure, I'll get it, but I know you're just sending me out of the room so I won't hear what you're going to say next." She shot a look at Zoe's arm. "But since you're hurt I'll let you get away with it this time." She turned and headed for the bathroom. Aaron lifted a brow, and Zoe's lips curved slightly even though her eyes didn't smile.

"You have your hands full with her, don't you?" Clay asked from his position near the kitchen door. Every once in a while he'd look out.

"A bit."

More than a bit, but she wouldn't trade raising Sophia for anything. She shook her head. "And no," she said to Aaron. "Sophia doesn't come with money attached. The only money I have is from the life insurance policy Trevor had taken out a couple of years ago. I think it's for two hundred fifty thousand dollars or something like that. Not enough to kill someone for."

Aaron lifted a brow. "You'd be surprised. Who's the beneficiary for your life insurance?"

"Sophia."

"And who gets Sophia if something happens to you again?"

"Nina. Trevor's sister." She raked her good hand through her tangled hair. She felt the color drain from her cheeks. "They would get custody and therefore control of the money and any other assets that I have."

"Here, Mom." Sophia came back into the kitchen carrying the first-aid kit.

Aaron took it from her. "Thanks."

"Can I watch?"

"You *may*. As long as it's okay with your mom." He shot a glance at Zoe and she nodded, her mind not on her arm, but on the deduction Aaron's questions had led her to.

Nina? Really? "It's okay," she murmured. She focused in on Sophia, her eyes automatically monitoring the color in her cheeks. She seemed all right, but she would check her sugar levels again in a bit.

Clay spoke into his phone then turned back. "That was Lance. They've cleared the area. The shooter is gone, but they found the place he shot from. A crime scene unit's on the way from Nashville to process the area. Lance said he doesn't want to assume anything, but he thinks the shooter is the one who got away. The one they called Jed."

"I think that's probably a safe assumption." Aaron cut the sleeve of her sweatshirt away from her arm then cleaned it up before pulling out a needle and suture thread. Zoe's eyes widened. "You're going to sew it up?"

"I carry the stuff for humans, too." He rolled his shirt up and showed her the scar on his left forearm. "Ever since I got tangled up with that angry bull last year, I make sure I can patch myself up if I need to."

"A bull did that?" Sophia asked.

"Nah, I got away from him. It was the rusty nail on the fence that got me when I went over. Sliced a big ole gash in my arm."

Sophia winced. "Wow. How bad did that hurt?"

"Big-time bad."

"So you're going to sew up Mom's cut?"

"Sure. If she wants me to." He looked at her and Zoe saw a gentle compassion there. And a willingness to let her make the call about her medical treatment. He wouldn't be offended if she refused to let him work on her arm. "Or," he said, "we'll just take her to the hospital and let another doctor do it."

"Aren't you a real doctor?" Sophia asked.

Aaron smiled. "The animals think so."

"It's fine," Zoe whispered. "I trust you." And she did.

Aaron sobered. "I have some numbing medicine. You'll only feel the first prick of the first needle."

"That's fine."

"Are you allergic to anything?"

"No, nothing."

The other officers milled around writing notes and recording every detail so when it came time to do the paperwork, everything would be right there and they wouldn't have to rely on memory. She watched them from the corner of her eye so she didn't have to see what he was doing.

Aaron worked quickly and efficiently and soon Zoe had a neat little row of five stitches in her upper arm. He'd been true to his word. Other than the initial prick of the first shot and a few slight tugs, she hadn't felt a thing. Sophia had never taken her eyes from him and his work on Zoe's arm, fascinated by the whole procedure.

Zoe's attention had been distracted anyway. She kept remembering the look on Aaron's face when she'd said she used to have a drug problem. She felt heat flush her face. Why had she told him that? And at that moment of all times? What was she thinking to let that kind of information loose when they'd been dodging bullets and fighting for their lives?

But other than his initial hesitation, he didn't seem fazed by the knowledge. She did think he'd bring it up again when they were alone. So now that she'd let the cat out of the bag, what was she going to tell him? The whole sordid story?

Yes. He deserved it. He was putting his life on the line for her, and she owed him nothing less than the absolute truth. She blew out a breath and tried to focus on her arm. Which wasn't hard. It throbbed with a fierce ache, but she'd deal with it. Without drugs.

Clay finally came back in and sat at the table. "How's the arm?"

Zoe drew in a deep breath. "Fine. Or it will be thanks to Aaron."

Clay nodded. "As you know, the shooter got away. We found some cartridges that tell us he was using a .45. Probably a rifle with a high-powered scope."

"I'm glad he missed." She looked at her arm. "Mostly missed anyway."

"Me, too. But…"

"But?"

"I don't think you're safe staying here, and I don't have the manpower to spare to protect you like you need it out here on the farm."

"So what are you saying, Clay?" Aaron asked as he repacked his supplies in the bag.

"I'm saying I think she needs to leave here. Go somewhere it will be easier to keep an eye on her. We can do this here at the ranch only on a short-term basis. If this situation is going to stretch out for any length of time then we need to come up with a better solution."

"Like what?" Aaron said.

"And where would I go?" she asked. "What about the animals?"

"I've already thought about the animals," Clay said. "We'll simply move the horses to our parents' ranch. There are plenty of hands to help take care of them. However, I don't think it's wise to take you and Sophia out there."

"No, of course not. We'd just bring trouble down on your family."

"It's not so much that as it is there's no place to put you. Mom and Dad have started renting out the cottages on the property again and they're all occupied right now—especially with Thanksgiving just around the corner."

"So what did you have in mind?" Aaron asked.

"Well, there are two options. One is Sabrina's grandmother's bed-and-breakfast. But that might be an issue if someone tried to get to Zoe there."

"No." Zoe lifted her chin and looked him in the eye. "I won't put any more innocent people in danger. You and Aaron and Lance are bad enough but at least you know how to defend yourselves."

He nodded. "I had a feeling you might feel that way. The other choice is also a place in town, right off the main street and across the street from the B and B. It's also near the sheriff's office. It's a small house, two bedrooms and one bathroom, but it's vacant. I recommend you and Sophia move there for now."

Zoe swallowed and looked at Aaron then back to Clay. "All right. If you think that's what we need to do, then we'll do it." And when she could think again, she'd see if she could figure out another place to run to. A place far away from Wrangler's Corner and the men who wanted her dead.

EIGHT

It had only taken Clay a matter of hours to get everything set up, but it wasn't until the next morning that they'd made the move. Clay had been fairly certain all of the activity at the Updike ranch would keep any would-be intruders away from the place for the duration.

He'd been right. Zoe had packed while Aaron got his folks' agreement to take the horses. The other lower maintenance animals would be fine as long as the weather cooperated and someone could come out once a day to care for them. Aaron would do it himself if he had to.

Now Zoe and Sophia were as comfortable as they could possibly be after having been held hostage, chased through the woods, shot at and then uprooted from their home away from home.

Two days after the incident, Aaron sat next to Lance in the cruiser and watched the front door of the house. The yellow home with green shutters and the wraparound porch was perfect according to Zoe. The only thing that made him slightly nervous was the door. It had a wood frame but was glass from top to bottom. And behind that door were two people he was coming to care for. Two people he had no business thinking about as much as he was. "It's been quiet," he said.

Lance nodded and took a bite of the sandwich Aaron had brought over to him. "I like it that way."

"I do, too, but it makes me nervous."

"I know what you mean." Lance glanced at him. "You're taking quite a bit of time away from your practice."

"Nah, I'm just making a few more house calls than usual. Nate's back from vacation and covering the office." Nathan Godfrey, his partner. "He and Jill had a fight so he's working extra hours to stay out of the line of fire."

Lance's jaw tightened. "Running away from your problems in a marriage won't do it much good."

Aaron nodded. Lance had been in a troubled marriage a couple of years ago. His wife had made a lot of rotten choices and had eventually died because of them. "I've never been married, but watching my parents and my siblings, I know that's the truth." He shrugged. "They'll work it out eventually."

"Whatever happened to that woman you were seeing a while back? I haven't noticed her around lately, but haven't had a chance to ask you about her."

Aaron winced. "Darla? She moved away about six months ago."

"Moved? As in permanently?"

"Yes."

"I'm sorry."

"Me, too." He glanced at the house again. "At least I was. I don't think about her much anymore." Of course if he consciously thought about it, he clearly remembered the sting of her betrayal. The heartache he'd felt when he realized she'd used him. And the anger. He never wanted to feel that kind of heartache again. Lance followed his line of sight. "She's a pretty special lady."

"You think?"

"I think *you* think so."

Aaron looked away. "Maybe." No maybe about it. Zoe was special. But he'd already decided he didn't want to get involved. Okay, correction. He did want to get involved, he wanted to take the time to explore the feelings she evoked in him every time he was around her, but he couldn't shake the fear of getting his heart broken again when she returned to her life in Knoxville. He simply wouldn't do it. And he wasn't sure he was open to a long-distance relationship. Maybe, though…if that was what Zoe wanted.

"What happened? Why'd she move away?"

"She didn't like living in a small town. She wanted to be in the city with the bright lights and," he said with a shrug, "I didn't." But he'd thought about it. Especially when she'd announced she was leaving town. In the end, she'd left and he'd stayed right where he'd always wanted to be. Home. With family and helping the good people of Wrangler's Corner. But Zoe was different. Could he put all that aside and follow Zoe to Knoxville? He wasn't sure. And she hadn't asked so he didn't know why he was even thinking along those lines anyway.

Ginny Garrison walked out the front door of the house and gave them a wave. Aaron climbed out of the cruiser and walked up the front steps to meet Ginny. "Is she ready?"

"Almost."

"Are you okay staying with Sophia?"

"Of course. She's a great kid."

"Thanks," Zoe said from behind Ginny. "She likes you, too."

Ginny smiled and backed up to let Aaron

inside. He took in Zoe's appearance and felt his heart thud an extra beat. She looked beautiful if still a bit pale. "Are you sure you're up to this?"

"I'm sure. It's my left arm that was hurt. I'm right-handed."

Yesterday, she'd requested a trip to the shooting range to brush up on her skills. She had a concealed weapon permit for the state of Tennessee but it had been awhile since she'd gone shooting.

Aaron hadn't been so sure the trip was a good idea, but he couldn't discount her reasons for wanting to do it. He led her to the cruiser. While Aaron was occupied with teaching her to shoot, Lance would be their eyes and ears on the surrounding area.

She slid into the backseat and Aaron took the front next to Lance. Lance glanced in the rearview mirror. "You used to shoot a lot?"

Aaron turned to see her nod. "Trevor and I used to go on the weekends to the shooting range. We used to try a lot of different guns. I've always enjoyed going to the range and have missed it since Trevor's been gone." She shrugged. "I just haven't had the heart to go." Her jaw firmed. "But I need to do this for Sophia and myself. I appreciate everything you all are doing, but I really need to be able to protect us."

No wonder she'd been so comfortable with the Winchester rifle at the Updikes'.

Small talk filled the car for the next hour until Lance turned onto a gravel drive that led to the parking lot of the shooting range. When Lance parked, Aaron climbed from the car and opened the door for Zoe. She slid out and he hustled her inside. Lance followed at a more sedate pace and Aaron knew he was checking out the surrounding area, watching the passing cars to see if any of them slowed or looked suspicious.

"Aaron, long time no see, man."

Aaron looked up to find Keith Nance, the owner of the place, behind the counter. "Hey there." Aaron led Zoe over and shook Keith's hand. "Good to see you." Keith was in his midsixties and still worked out an hour every day at the gym he'd built behind the shop. His bulging muscles attested to his dedication. "Keith, this is Zoe, a friend. She has her concealed weapon permit."

"But I need a little practice before I'll feel comfortable carrying again."

"You have a gun?" Keith asked her.

"No, I'll need to purchase one."

"That's not a problem. Do you have one

in mind?" He reached under the counter and pulled out a stack of paperwork and a pen.

"Something small and easy to carry in my purse or pocket, but one with a safety like the Smith & Wesson M&P Shield 9 mm. I have a child so I need the safety."

Aaron blinked. She knew her weapons. Keith appeared to be impressed, as well. "You've shot one before?"

"Yes."

"They're hard to keep, but I actually have one of those in stock. Got a shipment in two days ago." He went to the vault behind him and opened it.

He disappeared inside and Zoe looked at Aaron. "I left Knoxville so fast, I didn't think to get mine." She shook her head. "You would think that would have been the first thing I'd have gone after, but all I could think of was getting Sophia away, getting somewhere safe. I hadn't looked at that gun since Trevor died. It's still in a safe in the bedroom."

"It's understandable. You were probably in a state of shock, scared, not thinking straight."

She gave him a tremulous smile. "Yes. To all of the above."

When Keith came back, he held the small gun. "Here you go."

* * *

She nodded. "Perfect. Now, I just need an ankle holster and I'll be all set."

Zoe knew she'd surprised the men with her weapons knowledge, but Trevor had been an enthusiast and she supposed it had rubbed off on her. Then again, growing up on a small farm in the middle of nowhere, she'd handled rifles and pistols on a regular basis. One never knew when a rattlesnake might decide to take up residence in an empty barn stall or a wild wolf come looking for some lunch in the chicken coop. She'd been around guns her entire life.

Once she filled out the paperwork, she paid for the gun with her credit card. No sense in worrying about being traced by it. The bad guys already knew where she was. And maybe if they saw she'd purchased a gun, they'd think twice about coming back.

She doubted it, but one could hope.

Aaron led her back to the range, and Zoe was relieved they were the only ones there. She drew in a calming breath as she realized what she was doing. Preparing herself to defend herself and Sophia. Planning to shoot at someone if she had to. Shooting at targets was easy but could she really shoot at another human being? She prayed she wouldn't have to find out.

Zoe held the gun while Aaron opened the box of ammunition. He watched as she expertly loaded it. "I don't think you're going to need much practice."

She gave him a slight smile. "Probably not, but it's been over a year since I've handled a weapon."

He pressed the button to bring the target holder in. He clipped the paper with the black silhouette onto the holder and set it out about fifty feet. She slipped on the protective eyewear and inserted the earplugs.

He did the same and nodded. She lifted the pistol with her right hand, her left hand coming up to add support. She felt the stitches tug, but the pain was tolerable. Zoe closed one eye and focused on the target in front of her. Then pulled the trigger. Then pulled it again and again and again.

When she finished the last shot, she lowered the weapon. Aaron pressed the button to pull the target in close. Zoe's lips tightened as she studied it.

"You did great," Aaron said.

"A few wild shots, but a few center mass, too," she said. "Not too bad. Once I got the feel for the gun it all came back to me."

"Nice. Want to go again?"

"Sure."

Within a few minutes, she was back at it. With each round, her circle of holes in the paper got tighter and tighter.

"That's some good shooting, Zoe," Aaron said. "I'm impressed."

Zoe set the gun on the small bench in front of them and pulled her earplugs out. She could hear him okay, but he sounded muffled, like he was far away. She stared at the latest target with the holes. "I don't think I could shoot someone, Aaron."

"If it comes down to his life or yours, or his or Sophia's, I think you could."

Tears filled her eyes and she glanced up at him, not caring if he saw the wetness. "Yes, I could for Sophia." She sniffed, and a tear traced down her cheek. He lifted a hand and thumbed it away, but left his palm cupping her cheek. She drew in a sharp breath.

"Clay will figure out what's going on. The man in the hospital will wake up eventually, and Clay will get him to talk."

Zoe closed her eyes against the lovely sensation of his touch. She had no business feeling an attraction for him. Not when she was fighting for her and Sophia's lives. She opened her eyes and met his. "Aaron, I appreciate everything you and your family and friends have done for Sophia and me, but I think it's time for us to run again."

"How is that going to help?"

She sighed. "Well, for one, it'll give the authorities time to try and figure things out. But I can't run without help."

He frowned. "What do you mean?"

"I want you to help us disappear."

Aaron stared at her. At this beautiful woman he'd only known for a few weeks and yet felt incredibly drawn to. Drawn to against his better judgment for sure, but still he couldn't deny it. So once again he found himself falling for a woman who wasn't planning on sticking around but didn't mind using him to get what she needed. He was such a gullible idiot.

He withdrew his hand from her silky skin and drew in a deep breath even as he berated himself for feeling a depth of hurt that he had no business feeling. "Fine. You want to run? Run. Clay and Lance will help you get everything together." He grabbed her gun, made sure it was unloaded with the safety on and handed it to her. She stuffed the remaining bullets in her bag and shot him a troubled look.

The hurt in her eyes pierced him and Aaron immediately felt guilty. It wasn't her fault he had issues. "Ah, man. I'm sorry I snapped. Come on, let's get out of here."

"Aaron, what's wrong? What did I say?"

"Nothing." He couldn't get into it right here. The door opened and he tensed, but it was a young couple ready to take on the range. He and Zoe slipped around them and out into the store.

Lance looked over his shoulder from his position by the door. He took in Zoe's face then let his eyes connect with Aaron's. The question there made Aaron grimace. He shook his head and Lance frowned, but didn't say anything.

Aaron waited for Zoe to get in the car. She didn't look at him when he shut the door for her. Instead, she shoved the newly purchased weapon into her bag and clamped her lips tight. Aaron told himself not to let it get to him, but the hurt didn't go away.

"Is Sophia all right?" Zoe asked.

Lance nodded from his position behind the wheel. "I just talked to Ginny about five minutes before you came out of the range. Ronnie came by, and the three of them are together. Ginny said something about sugar-free s'mores in the fireplace."

Aaron glanced back at her and noticed her jaw loosen slightly. "Zoe wants to run, Lance, and she needs your help to do it." He forced the words out. If she wanted to leave, he'd help her. He wouldn't like it, but he'd help her. And then he might treat himself to a long vacation. Alone.

Lance raised a brow. "Is that right?"

"Yes," she said with a troubled look at Aaron. He avoided her gaze in the mirror. "It's the only thing I can think to do. I can't keep tying up the sheriff's department. Anyone who stays with us or is near us is in danger." Aaron's heart thawed slightly when her voice thickened. "I'm sorry, but I just don't know what else to do."

Lance nodded. "I understand. Let me run it by Clay and see what he thinks."

"Thanks," she whispered. Then closed her eyes and leaned her head against the window.

Aaron rubbed his chin and fell into silence while he wrestled with his thoughts. Lance drove with a quiet confidence and alertness that made Aaron feel glad the man had come with them. "So, why would you want to kidnap a kid and get rid of her mother?" he asked Lance in a low voice.

"Because there's some advantage. Something the kidnapper gets. Money? Highly likely." He grimaced. "There's the whole human trafficking thing, of course, but this feels like something more. Those men at the house were waiting on something. They were communicating with someone."

"Speaking of which, I wonder if Clay had any success tracing the numbers from Pete's phone."

"We'll be sure to ask him." He tapped his fingers on the wheel. "They didn't want Sophia hurt."

"It sure seemed that way. So it's someone who cares about Sophia, but not Zoe?"

"No, Zoe's obviously in the way."

"She said her sister-in-law offered to have them move in with her and her husband, but Zoe didn't want to. You think she could be forcing the issue?"

"It makes sense. Get rid of Zoe and get custody of Sophia—and get control of any money that might come with her."

"I don't think the motive is money," Zoe said.

Lance grunted. "I hate to tell you this, but it's almost always about money." His phone rang. "It's Clay." He pressed the Bluetooth button on the radio. "Hello."

"Lance, where are you?" Clay's voice filled the car.

"Still with Aaron and Zoe. What's up?"

"Our guy Pete is still out cold. He roused a bit and then went back under so he's no help right now. But I've been doing some digging into Trevor Collier."

Zoe stirred. "Trevor?"

"You found something?" Lance asked.

"Maybe. Looks like he had a thing for the horses."

"Gambling?"

A gasp came from the backseat, and Aaron turned to see Zoe shaking her head.

"Yeah," Clay said. "But I can't find that he ever lost that much. I mean his bank accounts are closed now, of course, but I was able to access them and there's nothing there to indicate it was an addiction."

"Maybe he was using someone else's money."

"He wasn't gambling," Zoe said. "He hated gambling."

"Then what was he doing at the tracks?" Clay's voice came over the speaker. "His buddies at the office said he was there most weekends."

"Like I told you earlier, Trevor was there to watch Thunderbolt race. He hated gambling, but he loved horses." She glanced at Aaron. "Trevor's grandmother had left him a trust fund and when she died he bought a horse with the money. The prestige of owning a winning horse was something he enjoyed. It was just fun for him." She shrugged. "A hobby that paid well."

"Paid well how?"

"Trevor got a percentage of every race the horse won, he allowed other people to pay him to use Thunderbolt in the hopes of producing winning offspring. There's a whole slew of ways a horse can generate income without gambling, you know this."

"Yes, but I wasn't sure that's what you meant."

"It was. Trevor went to the track on race days to support and encourage the jockey who was a good friend, almost like a son to Trevor. He just wanted to cheer him on. But Trevor didn't gamble. Ever."

"You hear that, Clay?" Lance asked.

"I heard it."

"But you don't believe me," Zoe said, her lips pressing into a flat line.

"It's not a matter of—"

Lance stiffened. "Hang on, Clay."

Aaron straightened. "What is it?"

"What is what?" Clay echoed.

Lance's fingers tightened around the wheel

and he looked back. "There's a car coming up fast on our rear."

They'd taken the back roads to Nashville instead of the highway thinking it would be easier to spot a tail than on the busy interstate. They were about thirty minutes outside of Wrangler's Corner on a two-lane road that ran between sprawling acres of land with private homes. The area was sparsely populated, but not isolated at all. Would someone really try something out in the open like this? Of course they would. "Looks like you were right to be concerned about someone following us."

Lance stepped on the gas, and the car surged forward just as a bullet shattered the back window.

NINE

Zoe screamed and ducked down into the seat, the seat belt sliding off her shoulder and allowing her to lie flat against the upholstery. All she could think was that she was grateful Sophia wasn't with her. She covered her head as the car swerved left then back right. "Stay down!" Lance hollered. Another pop, and the vehicle surged forward, limped a few paces then jerked to a stop. "Watch out, he shot out the tire and he's going to hit us!"

Zoe rose up and caught the flash of movement in the side window. When the slam came, she rocked to the side, hit the door with her shoulder. Ignoring the flash of pain, she gripped the door handle and held on.

Another crunch against the driver's side, then the teeth-grating screech of metal on metal. An engine revved, tires squealed.

Then silence.

Her heart pounded in her ears.

Then her seat belt flew off and hands clamped down on her upper arms and pulled. She let out a low scream. "It's me," Aaron said. "Come on. They shot out the tire, and we can't sit here."

Zoe scrambled out of the car, her arm throbbing when she pushed too hard with it. Aaron's grabbing it hadn't helped. She ignored it, knowing he hadn't meant to hurt her, and followed Aaron around to the side of the car. "How did he find us?"

"Who knows?"

Lance rounded the front of the car, his weapon drawn, face tight. "They drove off, but that doesn't mean they won't be back."

Aaron was already on the phone with Clay. Zoe listened, her mind spinning, blood still pounding through her veins with ferocious force. This was getting ridiculous. She was going to have to grab Sophia and disappear. She couldn't keep putting people in danger. Even if they were cops. But Aaron wasn't a cop. He'd just stumbled into this mess.

While Lance kept watch and Aaron held her against him, they waited, not wanting to leave the relative cover the vehicle provided. "What kind of car was it?" Aaron asked.

Lance glanced at him. "It was a dark blue

sedan. A Ford, I think. I got a partial plate, it was a Tennessee one. G34 something."

Sirens sounded in the distance but were closing the gap fast. Zoe let Aaron's warmth wrap itself around her. She shouldn't let him comfort her. She should move away, but she was so tired, so worn out, so scared...

Three police cruisers pulled to a stop, and the sirens cut off abruptly. Zoe slipped out of Aaron's arms. She heard Clay send two of the deputies to search the area but as she hugged her coat around her, she met Aaron's gaze and knew he was thinking the same thing she was. The shooter had escaped once again.

When Clay had finished taking all of the information the three of them could give him, he motioned for Joy to join them. She approached and Clay said, "Do you mind taking Zoe home? We've got to get a tow truck out here and get this scene cleaned up."

"Of course I don't mind." She smiled at Zoe. "Come on."

"I'll go with her," Aaron said.

"And I'm going to have Ronnie follow you to watch your back," Clay said. "We don't need a repeat of this." He lifted his notebook. "Now I'm going to go put this partial plate into the system and see if I can get a hit."

Zoe walked with Joy to the woman's

cruiser and slid into the backseat. She shut the door. Tremors shook her, and she knew it was from the adrenaline crash. She took a deep breath closed her eyes. Then opened them. She looked up to see Aaron standing there. "Want some company?"

"Are you still mad at me for wanting to leave?"

"No."

She scooted over, and he slid in beside her then wrapped an arm around her shoulder. She laid her head against him. "Why did you get so upset when I asked you for help?"

He glanced out the window, and she followed his gaze. Joy and Clay stood talking next to the driver's door.

"I had a bad experience, and your statement sort of brought it all back."

She shifted and looked up at him, into those eyes that she never grew tired of looking at. Probably why she dreamed about them sometimes at night. She blinked, pushing the thoughts away. "What happened?"

"I recently dated a woman named Darla. She and I knew each other from high school. We'd been good friends, hung out with the same crowd, that kind of thing. She eventually married a guy named Barry Foster. About four years into their marriage things turned ugly and she and Barry divorced. Anyway, about a year ago, she found a hurt puppy on the side of the road and brought him into my practice. She was sweet and we hit it off while catching up. I took her to dinner and we wound up in a relationship that I thought had the potential to lead to something permanent. Her son was a great kid." He looked away and swallowed. "But she had other plans. Apparently she knew as soon as Barry heard she was interested in someone else, he'd come crawling back. She kept pushing him away, toying with him, telling him she was going to marry me when she actually had no intention of doing so."

"Oh, my, how awful of her. I'm so sorry."

"Apparently she was just using me to teach Barry a lesson."

"Did it work?"

"I guess. She went back to him and the three of them moved out of town shortly after that."

"I'm sorry."

"It's okay. Now." He shot another glance out the window. Joy was writing something down. Zoe waited to see if Aaron had more to say. "When I first met you in town, I wanted to get to know you better, but you didn't seem interested." She looked away. She wasn't blind. She'd seen the spark of interest in his eyes and had felt a tug on her heart in response. She'd been interested, but also wary. He cleared his throat and placed a hand under her chin. "I'm just saying you're the first person I've looked at twice since Darla. The first person to capture my attention and I'm curious to see if…ah…that could grow into something. To put it awkwardly, but there you go."

She let out a low shaky laugh. "Wow. You just kind of lay it out there, don't you?"

He gave a derisive chuckle. "Not usually, but I want you to understand so I'm trying to make sure I'm pretty clear. I'm saying that my feelings have a lot to do with why I reacted so strongly. I don't want you to leave." He sighed. "But I'm not a completely selfish moron. I do want you to be safe."

She frowned. "I want that, too. I've grown to love Wrangler's Corner and the people who live here, but someone is out to kill me and take my daughter away. I just don't know what else to do." She felt like a broken record.

"We'll figure it out." He leaned over and kissed the top of her head, and her pulse shifted into overdrive. "I'll help you do whatever you need to do."

"Thank you," she whispered just as Joy opened the driver's-side door and climbed in.

"Did you find anything out?" Aaron asked.

"Not much. We matched the plate with the car and it came back as stolen. But the home it was taken from has security cameras around the perimeter so we might get a hit from one of those."

"I'm not holding my breath."

"Yeah, I wouldn't, either."

The ride back to town was silent and calm, but Zoe's tension didn't ease until the small house came into view. It looked like a haven, an oasis in her world gone mad. It was exactly the kind of house she would have chosen to buy had she been looking. But she wasn't. She was hiding out, praying whoever was after her and Sophia would either give up and go away or be caught.

However, for now, she was thankful to be alive, grateful for the friends who'd taken it upon themselves to protect her and Sophia. Especially the man beside her. Her mind lingered on Aaron's story—and from the pensive look on his face, he was thinking about hers.

When he'd told her his experience, he hadn't tried to hide the pain he'd suffered, hadn't tried to brush it off as no big deal. He'd let her see him, who he was deep inside. And that made her want to get to know him even more. One reason she'd been able to open up about her past and her struggle with the addiction. Even now, some days the desire to use something to escape reality prodded her, but thanks to coping strategies and thoughts of her daughter, she was able to resist. Getting to know Aaron on a deeper level would just make leaving harder.

But if running meant keeping Sophia safe then she'd do what she had to do. And that might just break her heart.

The next two days passed without incident, which just made Zoe's nerves stretch tighter and tighter until she thought they'd surely snap if she even moved wrong.

Sophia had an escort to and from school and someone with her at all times while on campus. Letting Sophia out of her sight kept Zoe on pins and needles until her child was back safe, but Sophia enjoyed the interaction with the other children and needed it. She needed for her life to feel normal. So while it was her desire to smother her child and keep her close, she'd decided to trust the people helping her. To a point.

Zoe couldn't help but stay tense, constantly wondering when the other shoe was going to drop. Now that she didn't have the animals to take care of, she spent her days alternating between racking her brain, searching for a reason someone would want to kill her, and painting. She still took online orders and didn't want to get too far behind. Customers were counting on her to get the paintings done in a timely manner for gifts.

Zoe walked into the small sunroom and stared at her half-finished painting. She studied the photograph then picked up her brush. Swift strokes finished the newborn's rosy cheeks and long lashes. Zoe glanced at the clock then moved into the kitchen to sit on the bar stool in front of the open laptop.

The gun felt heavy in her ankle holster, but after the latest incident, she wouldn't be caught without the weapon.

She finished the last bite of her club sandwich and clicked on the link that would take her to the email detailing the transaction of the horse she and Trevor had purchased together. This morning, she'd been getting Sophia ready for school when Ginny had picked up the newspaper and said something about the local winter bazaar that was to be next weekend with vendors and every kind of food available. And pony rides.

The mention of the pony rides had made Zoe think of the conversation in the car about Trevor and the horses. They thought he'd been gambling, but he hadn't been. She would have known because she kept up with the money and their bank accounts. He could have used money from his business, she supposed, but there'd never been any hint that anything had been amiss there. She thought she'd been clear about that fact when they'd all been at the house for breakfast, but figured they had to do their own investigation, their own digging for facts. And while she appreciated the thoroughness, she hated that they'd wasted time that could have been spent going in another direction.

She scanned the email that contained all of the documents that pertained to the purchase of Thunderbolt. She read it again, but nothing looked any different than the first time she and Trevor had gone over it together.

A knock on the door brought her head up, and she stood but allowed Joy to answer it. Joy kept a hand on her weapon while she looked out the window. Then her tense posture relaxed. "It's Aaron."

Two little words that sent Zoe's heart beating a little faster. Anticipation leaped inside her, and she curled her fingers into fists. She really had to put this whole attraction thing aside. Unfortunately her heart had other ideas. She wanted to bolt to the foyer mirror and check her hair and what little makeup she'd applied this morning, but resisted.

Aaron stepped inside and gave her a small smile. "Hi."

"Hi."

"I had a break at the clinic so thought I'd come by and see how you were doing."

She shrugged. "I'm hanging in there."

"I'll be in the study," Joy said. She disappeared through the open door to the left, and Zoe appreciated the deputy's discretion.

She led Aaron into the kitchen and gestured to the computer. "I'm just trying to figure out who's behind all this and if our purchase of Thunderbolt had anything to do with it."

"Any success?"

"Not really. Although for some reason I keep coming back to the conversation in the car about Trevor and the racetrack." She shook her head. "I know Trevor wasn't gambling, though, so it's not that he owed people money. Clay and Lance have already determined that. I thought maybe there was some detail in the purchase agreement that I'd missed, but I can't see anything out of the ordinary."

Aaron sat on the stool next to her. "Where's the horse?"

She ran her palms down her jeans. Being around him always seemed to make her hands sweat and her pulse kick it up a notch. "He's boarded at a barn in Knoxville where the monthly fee is drafted from an account set up especially for that. The jockey, Brian Cartee, goes by the stable and rides the horse on a regular basis and then races him during the season. Any money generated is automatically deposited back into the same account. Brian's crazy about that horse and spends as much time as possible with him. It's a wonderful arrangement." She shook her head. "Trevor was like a father to Brian. Brian was devastated when Trevor was killed in the accident."

"What happens to the horse if something happens to you?"

She frowned. "You think this is about the horse, too?"

"I don't know. How much is he worth?"

She stared at him, her brain whirring. "A lot," she whispered. "The last time Trevor checked he said Thunderbolt was valued at a quarter of a million."

Aaron's eyes widened. "That is a lot."

She pressed her thumb and forefinger against her eyes as she thought. Then she looked up. "Yes, it is a pretty good chunk of change, isn't it? So it could be someone after the money that Thunderbolt would bring. Why not just steal the horse?"

"Have you ever tried to sell a black market horse?"

She wrinkled her nose and frowned. "Of course not."

"Thunderbolt's a well-known horse in the racing arena. He'd be recognized as soon as he got to the tracks."

She pondered that. "True."

"So who gets control of the horse if something happens to you?" he asked again.

"He goes to Sophia."

"And Sophia goes to…"

"… Nina and Gregory," she said. "It keeps coming back to them, doesn't it?"

"I'm afraid so."

She shook her head. "I don't believe it. They don't need the money. Gregory makes a very comfortable living as an attorney, and Nina can't keep up with all of the interior design requests she gets. And besides, Nina is crazy about Sophia. She'd never take a chance on her being hurt."

"Well, the plan was to hurt you, not Sophia, right?"

"That's what it looks like, yes, but still…" Her frown deepened. "You know, something else just occurred to me."

"What?"

"When the men first showed up at the ranch, one of them, Pete, had Sophia by her hair and was pointing his gun at her. When I started to go toward him, he lifted the gun and aimed it at me." She shuddered. "I could see it in his eyes. He was going to shoot me right there in front of my child. I dove and he pulled the trigger. Then the other man came out of the house, the one they called Cody. He yelled at Pete to stop shooting. At first I thought he was there to rescue us, but he wasn't, of course. But he said they couldn't kill me. Not yet."

"So they need you for something."

"I guess."

"So shooting at us and running us off the road weren't attempts to kill you, but to *get* you?"

She shrugged. "It's the only thing I can really come up with."

"Now I'm confused. If they simply manage to kill you, everything goes to Sophia and Sophia goes to your sister-in-law and her husband."

"Along with control of any assets that I have."

"You didn't leave anything for your parents or your brother?"

"No," she snapped. "Why would I?"

"There's a lot of bitterness in those words," he noted quietly.

She drew in a deep breath and stood. Paced into the living area that connected to the kitchen. The open floor plan would allow Aaron to keep his gaze on her. She could feel it boring into her back. She stopped at the mantel that held two pictures. One of her and Sophia, and one of her and Trevor and Sophia as a newborn.

She got a grip on her emotions. "I'm sorry, I didn't mean to sound bitter. I had a very trying childhood. I've made peace with it. Mostly. But I don't want to talk about that right now." She waved a hand in dismissal of the subject. "Trevor and I talked and he set everything up that way anyway. I didn't argue with him." She paused. "Although I will say that if I knew where my brother was, I'd include him in my will."

"Well, maybe Clay or Lance needs to pay a visit to Nina and Gregory."

She rubbed her eyes. "I don't know. Maybe."

His phone rang, and he snagged it from the clip on the side of his jeans. "Excuse me. It's Clay."

"Sure."

"Hello?" She watched him while he listened. He had faint lines at the corners of his eyes, probably from squinting into the sun. His skin was tanned even in November and his firm jaw spoke of strength, not just physical, but an indication of his character. Something she'd already seen in action. And then his full lips flattened and his cheeks whitened beneath the tan. "Okay. Thanks for letting me know. I'll see you when you get here." He hung up and stared at the wall without blinking.

"Aaron?"

"He's dead."

She blinked. "Who?"

"Pete. The guy I shot."

TEN

Zoe let out a low gasp. Aaron slid off the stool and made his way over to the couch where he dropped onto the cushion and let his hands dangle between his knees. His chin rested on his chest and he stared at the floor. Zoe came to sit beside him. "I thought he was going to be okay."

"So did I." He rubbed his eyes. "There'll be an autopsy, of course."

"Did he ever wake up?" she asked.

"No." Her shoulders slumped, and he wrapped an arm around her and drew her to him. At first she resisted then she let him. He ignored the warning his brain sent his heart. He'd known her a very short time, but already he was finding ways to weave her and her child into his life, keenly aware of the possibility that he might be setting himself up for a hard and painful fall. He swallowed as another fact hit him. "I killed a man."

She looked up. "Oh, Aaron, I'm so sorry."

He shook his head. "It's sad. I'm sad, but I couldn't let him hurt Lance."

"Of course you couldn't. If you hadn't shot Pete, Lance would be dead."

"I know. I realize that of course, but it's still..." He rubbed a hand down his cheek and knew she was right. It wasn't that. He just didn't have the words to explain the feeling. And he knew that if he could go back in time to the very moment he pulled the trigger, he'd have to do it again. Pete hadn't given him a choice.

Her arms slid around his neck, and she laid her head on his chest. His breath caught and he closed his eyes, wishing things were very different. He placed a finger under her chin and lifted it until her lips were a fraction of an inch from his. And then he kissed her. A slow tender exploration that didn't last nearly as long as he wanted. She didn't resist, but he could feel her hesitation. When he lifted his head, she opened her eyes and looked into his. "Is this wise?" she whispered.

"Probably not." Actually, it was definitely not. "But I won't apologize. The more time we spend together, the more I feel..."

"I know, I feel the same, but—" she looked away then back "—I'm not staying in Wrangler's Corner forever, Aaron," she whispered. "Just until this is over." She shook her head. "And maybe not even until then. I have a life to get back to. A business. A family. Of sorts. They're my in-laws, but they've been good to me." She gave a soft grunt. "Better than my blood family."

"Yeah. I know." He'd managed to convince her to stay this long, but every time he knocked on her door, he half expected to find her gone. The uncertainty was playing havoc with his emotions, and he knew he'd have to make a decision soon about keeping his heart out of the equation. He ignored the little voice that mocked him, insisting it was too late. He cleared his throat. "Clay's on his way over. He said he wanted to talk to you about the phone calls traced back to Pete's phone. He should be here any minute."

She sniffed and nodded. "All right."

"How's Sophia handling everything?"

"She's still doing okay. She sleeps in my bed these days, and I let her. If I thought it would be best for her, I'd keep her shackled to my side, but I don't want her living in fear. I have to admit, though, letting her go to school is one of the hardest things I do."

"She likes school."

"Yes. She's made some sweet friends. And

she really likes it here in Wrangler's Corner—minus the people shooting at us and chasing us."

The knock on the door brought Joy from the study, her hand on her weapon. Again, she relaxed after looking out the window. "It's Clay." She opened the door and let him in. He stepped into the foyer and pulled his gloves off. A light dusting of snow fluttered to the floor.

"It's snowing again," Clay said.

"You're kidding," Aaron deadpanned.

Clay rolled his eyes and then frowned. "How are you holding up?"

Aaron sobered. "I'm processing."

Clay's attention turned to Zoe. "I can't stay long. I need to get back to Sabrina, but wanted to stop by and check on you as well as let you know that I got some information."

"You could have called."

Clay shrugged. "Yeah, I could have."

"You're restless and it feels good to have something to do other than pace?"

Clay grimaced. "You always could see beneath the surface."

Aaron slapped his brother on the shoulder. "What have you got?" Aaron asked.

"First, as you know, the car we got the partial plate on came back stolen from just outside of Knoxville and hasn't been recovered yet. We've got a BOLO on it so hopefully one of our deputies will spot it."

"You said 'first.'"

"We also got some information from the phone Pete used."

Zoe leaned forward. "What kind of information?"

"The phone itself was a burner, not traceable as to who purchased it, et cetera, however, we checked all the numbers, incoming and outgoing. He'd erased almost all of the numbers, but one was interesting."

"Who?" Zoe whispered. Aaron clasped her cold fingers in his warm ones.

Clay pursed his lips then blew out a low breath. "There was one call that came in about the time you were being held hostage by the three men on the Updike farm."

"From who?" Aaron demanded.

"The Bishop residence in Knoxville, Tennessee."

The room spun for a moment before Zoe drew in a deep breath and commanded herself not to pass out. "It can't be," she whispered. "I don't believe it. Nina's always been a little overbearing and selfish, but there's no way she or Gregory would send killers after me. They have no reason to."

"Knoxville is a good two-hour drive from here," Clay said. "I'm going to send Lance and Parker to question them."

"We can't just call them?"

He shook his head and Zoe heard his phone buzz. "I want the element of surprise, and I want their reactions carefully noted." He glanced at his phone and his eyes widened. "That was a text from Mom. I've got to get to the hospital. Sabrina's in labor."

Zoe gasped. "Then get out of here. You have to go."

"I am. My mother and Sabrina's grand-mother are with her. I think Seth and Tonya are arriving in a couple of hours so it's going to be a bit crazy." His eyes narrowed and he looked at Zoe. "But don't think I'm lowering my guard when it comes to your and Sophia's safety. Joy checked in just a few minutes ago and said all was well."

"Good." Zoe nodded. "But you need to go. Give Sabrina my best. You're going to be a great dad."

Clay swallowed and paled slightly, but the joy in his eyes was unmistakable. "Well, I do have three children already," he mumbled. "It's not like I don't know what being a dad means." He looked at Zoe. "Sabrina and I adopted three."

Aaron cleared his throat. "This is his first birth, though," he said to Zoe. He turned his gaze back to Clay. "I've never seen you this spooked."

Clay snorted. "I'm not spooked." He blinked against a suspicious moisture Zoe thought she saw in his eyes, but decided she must have been mistaken when he shot his brother a hard look. "I just don't want anything to happen to them."

Aaron softened and pushed all kidding aside. "They'll be fine. You've been waiting for this for a long time."

"Yeah. Lance is in charge while I'm with Sabrina. If you need anything get in touch with him. He knows how to get a hold of me if he needs me." The two brothers hugged, and then Clay slipped out the door.

Aaron shut it behind him.

"He's terrified," Zoe mused.

"Yes, he is. Not of being a dad or taking care of a baby, but more that something could go wrong with the birth. I don't know how he would survive that." Aaron drew in a deep breath and shoved his hands into his pockets.

"Are you all right?"

"Like I told Clay, I'm still processing the

fact that Pete died, but in the end, I'll be okay. He made his choices and I had to make mine."

She moved back into the living area, and he followed. "Aren't you going to the hospital?" she asked.

"Babies take a while to get here. I'm not in a huge hurry." She nodded and he sat on the couch and leaned his head back. Staring at the ceiling for a moment, he said nothing. She let him have his quiet moment. Finally he looked at her and asked, "Are you okay? That was some pretty shocking news Clay just delivered."

She rubbed her temple. "Am I okay? No, not really. I don't understand why Nina or Gregory would have anything to do with this." She pursed her lips. "So what's the next step? What do we do?"

"Like Clay said, Lance and Parker will pay them a visit along with someone from the local police force. He may subpoena phone records, financial statements..." He shrugged. "That sort of thing."

"You sure know a lot about investigations. Did you get that from listening to Clay?"

"Clay and Stephen."

"Where is Stephen now? I haven't heard anything about him recently."

He realized she didn't know about his brother Stephen's death. "Amber didn't tell you?"

"Tell me what?"

"Before Clay took over, Stephen was the sheriff here in Wrangler's Corner. He was killed when he got too close to a drug ring."

She paled. "No, she didn't tell me. We haven't really spoken much. Just an email exchange here and there. I'm so sorry to hear that."

He nodded. "His death hit us all hard. Clay came home from Nashville where he'd been working as a detective. He solved Stephen's murder, and while we're glad for the closure, we still miss him."

"I'm sure." She lifted her chin. "I want to go with them."

"What?"

"To Knoxville. If Lance goes to confront my sister-in-law and brother-in-law, I want to go."

He frowned. "I don't think that's a very good idea."

"Maybe not, but I want to see their faces and hear their words for myself."

He gave a slow nod then checked his phone and rose. "I'll tell Clay. I guess I need to get going. I don't want to miss the birth of my nephew or niece."

"Let me know how it goes."

"Of course." He paused. "Do you want to come?"

"I'd better not. I don't want to take a chance that whoever is after me will follow us to the hospital or something. You go. Celebrate this time with your family."

He lifted a hand to cup her cheek. When she didn't pull away he leaned over to place a light kiss on her lips. She blinked up at him. "At some point we're going to talk about what's going on between us, right?" he asked.

She gave a little sigh. "There's definitely something there, isn't there?"

"Definitely."

"When this is all over, we'll talk." She frowned. "Assuming I'm still alive."

He scowled. "You'll still be alive. If I have anything to say about it, you'll still be alive." He kissed her again. This time a little longer, and now she felt the hint of desperation he couldn't quite hide.

When he lifted his head, her eyes glittered with unshed tears. "I hope you're right, Aaron. I really hope you're right."

She shut the door behind him and pressed cold fingers to her warm lips. "What are you doing, Zoe?" she whispered. "Don't put your heart on the line, it'll just get broken. Not only that, you'll break his, too."

"What?"

Zoe spun to find Joy in the doorway between the kitchen and the foyer. Zoe gave a low laugh. "Nothing. Just talking to myself."

"Anything you want to share?"

"No. It's all right." Or it would be if she could follow her own advice and keep Aaron at arm's length. She had to.

She glanced at the clock. She had a couple of hours before Ginny would bring Sophia home. "I'm going to make a few phone calls."

"Sure thing. I'm just going to walk the perimeter of the house, take a look around."

"All right."

Joy slipped out the front door, and Zoe returned to the computer. Her cell phone lay on the table next to the mouse. She picked it up and scrolled through her list of contacts. When she came to Nina Bishop, she stopped. And pressed the button. It rang once. Twice.

Zoe hung up.

Clay had said he wanted the element of surprise, and she couldn't interfere. She rubbed her eyes. That had been dumb. She shouldn't have pressed the button.

Thankfully, Nina wouldn't recognize the

number. Zoe had bought a disposable phone at the first stop on her way out of town. But still…

She set the phone back on the table. She and her sister-in-law had never been best friends, but they'd always gotten along and chatted amicably when they'd been together for holidays or birthdays. Did Nina have it in her to be a part of a plan to kill her? Zoe couldn't fathom it but couldn't deny it sure looked like it.

Restless, she stood and paced to the window. She stood to the side as she'd been taught and looked out. From her angle, she could see Sabrina's grandmother's bed-and-breakfast. A large white house that had been built in the late eighteen hundreds. It looked quiet. Deserted. The whole street was almost eerily vacant. She shuddered and tried to put a lid on her overly active imagination. Then again, who could blame her for seeing the possibility of danger at every turn?

With a low growl of frustration, she grabbed her phone and powered up her e-reader application. She scrolled through the novels. "No mysteries, thank you. I need a comedy."

She settled on one, curled up on the couch and began to read until her eyes grew heavy.

The slamming door jerked her from the light doze she'd slipped into.

"Mom?"

"In here, Sophia."

Sophia ran into the den and dropped her backpack on the floor near the recliner then climbed in Zoe's lap. Zoe buried her nose in her child's hair then kissed her cheek. "How was your day?"

"It was good. Very exciting."

"Really?" Zoe shot a look at Joy who hovered in the doorway. Joy raised her brows and gave a slight smile. Zoe's pulse slowed slightly.

"Yes," Sophia enthused. "Gordon brought a frog to school. It was part of his science project, but then Leon opened the cage and the frog jumped out. All the other girls screamed, but I helped catch it." She shot Zoe a brilliant smile. "And then Gordon hugged me and said I was awesome for a girl."

Zoe released a slow breath and sent up a silent prayer of thanks. Finally, her child was acting like a child, not the solemn miniature adult she'd become ever since the *first* kidnapping attempt. "You are awesome. Period." Her phone buzzed, and she snagged it. Aaron. To Sophia, she said, "Why don't you go get your snack out of the refrigerator? It's time for you to eat a little something." Sophia nodded and skipped into the kitchen. Zoe raised the phone to her ear. "Hello?"

"Hi, Zoe." Aaron's voice rumbled sweetly in her ear. "Just thought I'd let you know that baby girl Starke is here. When she decided it was time to enter the world, she did it fast, kicking and screaming. Nothing wrong with that kid's lungs, that's for sure."

"Oh, that's so great! And everyone is doing well?"

"Just perfect."

She smiled at the excitement in his voice. He'd be a great uncle. "What's baby girl's first name?"

"They haven't decided yet. Apparently that's been up for discussion for a few weeks." He cleared his throat. "Lance came by, and he and Parker are going to Knoxville to talk to your sister-in-law tomorrow."

"Tell them I want to go."

"I really think you need to stay here under protection with Sophia and Ginny and Joy."

She considered his words. She was touched that he was so concerned. The deep caring in his voice made her heart flutter and anxiety bit her. She was going to break his heart if she wasn't careful. Or vice versa.

But he might be right. If her sister-in-law

and her husband were behind the attempts on her life, did she really want to face them? But what if they weren't responsible? What if she left Sophia and something happened? "All right, I'll stay here."

"Good. I think that's a wise decision."

She heard him gasp.

"What is it?" she asked.

"My sister, Amber, just walked in."

"Oh! Tell her I said hello."

"Okay, I'll talk to you later." She hung up and leaned her head against the wall and tried to calm her racing heart. She was thrilled for Clay and Sabrina and the Starke family. A baby was a beautiful thing. Sophia came back into the den with her peanut-butter sandwich and settled herself on the couch beside Zoe. Zoe ran a hand over her child's hair and Sophia snuggled into her side. Yes, a baby was a beautiful thing. And so was her nine-year-old daughter that someone wanted to kidnap. Her throat tightened. And the prayer slipped out. *Please, God, keep us safe.*

ELEVEN

Aaron clapped Clay on the back. "Congratulations, big brother."

"Thanks. I have to say that was the most amazing thing ever. Well, second to Sabrina agreeing to marry me. Actually, they're neck and neck."

Aaron grinned then moved aside to let his sister take her turn at hugging Clay and admiring their new niece. When she stepped back, he caught her hand. "You've missed too many family milestones. Glad you could make it for this one."

Her mouth smiled, but her eyes remained shuttered. "I am, too, Aaron. I don't miss them because I want to."

He narrowed his eyes. "What's going on with your job?"

She blinked. "What do you mean?"

He shook his head. "Are you really a travel writer?"

"Of course."

The lack of expression made him wonder, but he didn't have time to get into it with her.

Lance waved Aaron over, and he gave his sister one last hug just in case she took off without saying goodbye as she'd been known to do.

He joined Lance who led him outside of the room. "What is it?"

"Just wanted to let you know we did a little digging into Zoe's in-laws and biological family."

"What did you find?"

Lance referred to his phone. "When we dug into the Bishops, Zoe's in-laws, red flags started waving."

"What'd you find?"

"You know how Zoe said they weren't hurting for money? That they had no reason to harm her or try to get Sophia?"

"Yes."

"Turns out that's not quite true."

Aaron stiffened. "What do you mean?"

"Seems they've fallen on rough times financially."

"Meaning what exactly?"

"They're not in bankruptcy or anything, but they're in debt and obviously struggling.

The creditors are going to start lining up pretty soon."

Aaron blew out a low breath. "So that gives them some motive for wanting to get their hands on the horse."

"That's the way I see it. They know Zoe isn't worth much. The only real money she has is tied up in that horse."

"So if they get rid of her, they get Sophia and the horse. They sell the horse for a quarter million and keep the money. That would pay quite a few bills."

Lance rubbed the back of his head. "That's what I'm thinking. We're still investigating, but it's not looking good for the Bishops."

"What about her biological family? Were you able to track them down?" Aaron glanced through the open door at his parents. There were completely enamored with the baby girl as were Clay and a beaming Sabrina. He wanted to be in the midst of them, but he just couldn't let this go. He needed to help Zoe figure this out.

Lance nodded. "There could be some motive there, but their contact with each other has been so sporadic over the years, it's hard to tell. Here's what I do know. Her dad is a real winner. He was an accountant for a large firm in Nashville. He was caught embezzling from the company funds and was arrested when Zoe was thirteen years old. He spent three years in prison. When he got out, he came home to divorce papers, but didn't actually move out until about a year after that."

"Nowhere to go?"

"Or didn't want to go and refused to."

"What about Zoe's mother? She let him stay there?"

"Not sure he gave her a choice. The divorce wasn't final for a long time so he may have just refused to sign the papers. I could track down the lawyer and find out if we need to. It's weird. Zoe disappeared without a trace for about a year shortly after he got out and went home, then resurfaced to get her GED. She went on to college and excelled. She got her degree in zoology and worked in a local zoo for a while before she married her husband. After that, she was a stay-at-home mom and now a widow."

Aaron sucked in a deep breath then let it out slowly. "A widow on the run from a killer."

"Yes."

"And you don't know where she was for that year?"

"Nothing came up on the original search,

but there are other ways to find out stuff like that. It may take me a while, but I can do it."

"What about her brother?"

"His name is Tobias Potter," Clay said. "He fell off the grid around the age of twenty-one, and there's nothing I can find on him."

"Does he have a record?"

"Nope."

Aaron rubbed a hand across his chin as he processed the information. "Weird that both of them disappeared."

Clay nodded. "Are you going to ask her about it?"

"Yes."

"Want me to look into it?" Amber asked.

Aaron jumped. "Still sneaky, aren't you, sis?"

She lifted a brow, innocence radiating from her. "What do you mean?"

"You know what I mean. But what do *you* mean that you could look into it?"

She shrugged. "I do a lot of travel articles, you know that. I also do some investigative pieces every once in a while. As a result I've got contacts in…um…some influential places. I can make a few calls."

"You were roommates. Why would you have to make some calls?"

Amber flushed. "Yes, we were roommates,

but we weren't superclose friends." She held up a hand. "And before you start casting blame on me, Zoe was very tightfisted with her past." She shrugged. "And I didn't push it. We talked mostly about things in the present, and she didn't share much about her past at all. Now. Do you want me to make the calls or not?"

Aaron cocked his head, fighting to keep his skepticism from showing. "What kind of calls?"

"Productive ones. Yes or no?"

"Yes," Aaron said, still watching her eyes. They gave nothing away.

She nodded and walked away.

Aaron looked back at Lance. "Do you ever get the feeling there's more to her than meets the eye?"

"What do you mean?"

Aaron shook his head "Some things just don't add up with her." He grimaced. He didn't have time to dwell on his quirky sister right now. "Whatever. Maybe she can come up with something. I'm going to head back to the office then I hope to swing by Zoe's before going home."

"Ginny and Joy are there. Ginny has to leave, but Joy will be there all night."

"Good." Aaron waved at his mother who

had the baby snuggled up against her. "And let me know if they come up with a name, will you?"

"Of course."

Aaron sent a text to Zoe letting her know his plans and checking with her. She responded: Everything is quiet here. Plan to stay for dinner with us if you like. See you soon.

While Sophia watched a video in the den, Zoe put the finishing touches on the dinner. Aaron would arrive at any moment and her heart wouldn't stop fluttering like a butterfly trapped in her chest. On the one hand, she'd almost forgotten how wonderful it felt to anticipate the attention of a man, an admirer. On the other hand, she really had to quit thinking about him as a potential boyfriend. He'd made his interest clear, but her life was too crazy to commit to anything right now, even dating. And Aaron deserved more than a "maybe."

Still…he was coming to her house, and she was excited to see him. Every minute they spent together drew them closer, and she was selfish enough to admit she didn't want to give that up.

She checked in on Sophia who looked up

from the television. "Is Doctor Aaron going to be here soon?"

"Soon."

Sophia smiled, and her eyes twinkled their eagerness to see her friend. Zoe went back to the kitchen. Aaron had completely captured her child's heart, and she wasn't far behind. She gulped and stirred the mashed potatoes, checked the rolls and opened the oven to poke the chicken. Almost ready. And nothing left to do with her hands. She clasped them in front of her and tried to imagine a life without fear, without danger—without Aaron. The last part hurt, and she knew she was in trouble. Not just the physical kind, but the emotional kind. So what was she going to do?

"Something smells good in here."

She turned to find Ginny in the doorway. "Thanks. I made enough for you and Joy, too."

Ginny's eyes widened. "Really?"

"Really."

"Wow, that's so nice of you, but Joy is going to stay the night and I'm going to be back first thing in the morning. Do you think I could get a to-go plate?"

Zoe laughed. "Of course."

"Could I ask you a question?"

Zoe tilted her head. "Of course."

"You've shared a little about your family with me and I understand that you're estranged, but is there no one that you could have turned to during this time? To help protect you, I mean? No other friends?"

Zoe sighed and stirred the beans—that didn't need stirring—while she tried to decide how she wanted to answer that. "No, not really. Like I've explained, my family isn't close. And quite frankly, I haven't wanted to take a chance on putting anyone else in danger."

"What about your in-laws? Nina and Gregory or your father-in-law?"

Zoe stared at the deputy. Ginny gave a little laugh. "Sorry, but Sophia's quite a talker. I feel like I know each member of the Collier and Bishop families very well."

Zoe blew out a little breath and laughed as she pulled a paper plate and some tin foil from the pantry. "Sophia is definitely a talker." She rubbed her nose and considered her words. "I suppose I could have asked my father-in-law," she finally said. "He's a hard man to get to know, but I like him. He's always been very generous to me. Even after Trevor died." She shrugged and spooned the food onto the plate then covered it with the foil. "And I know he loves Sophia but like I said, I didn't feel like I could put him and the others in danger, you know?"

"So he offered to help?"

"Yes. And truthfully, maybe I should have accepted it, but I just didn't want anyone to know where we were until I could figure out what to do. If we'd stayed with him or even my sister-in-law and her husband, whoever was after Sophia would still know where she was. I didn't want that."

"Why don't you call him and ask him to help you now?"

Zoe frowned. "For the same reasons. I don't want to bring this trouble, this danger, into their lives. I've thought about it many times, but am trying to be patient and let Clay and Lance and all of you do your job." She rubbed her forehead. "Or maybe I should just go to him. It sure would make things easier on you guys, wouldn't it?"

"Maybe. It sounds like he would do anything to protect you."

"He would."

Ginny shrugged. "So why not call him?"

Zoe stared out the window. "No. Not yet. I'm not ready to do that yet."

"I understand." Ginny smiled. "Thanks for letting me be nosey."

"Any time." Zoe handed Ginny the plate, and the deputy grinned.

"Thanks," Ginny said. "I'll see you in the morning."

"I'll be here."

Joy stuck her head in the kitchen. "I think there's someone snooping around outside. I'm going to take a look. Ginny, you stay with her, all right?"

And there it was. The reminder that not all was well in her world. Zoe stiffened and watched Ginny instantly go from wide-eyed hungry woman to a trained professional. Ginny practically threw the plate onto the counter then went after her coworker.

"Wait!" Zoe called and made it into the foyer in time to find Joy halfway out the door and Ginny standing with her hand on her weapon. "Aaron's on his way over. He should be here any minute." She pulled her phone from her pocket. "I'll try to reach him and let him know what's going on, but just watch for him."

"I'll be careful. Lock the door behind me," Joy said. And then she was gone, shutting the door behind her. Zoe dialed Aaron's number with one hand and locked the door with her other. She felt her nerves rise to the surface of her skin. His phone rang four times then went to voice mail. "Aaron, if you get this, be careful around my house. Someone was outside, and Joy is looking for him." She hung up and dialed again.

"Mom?"

She turned, phone pressed to her ear, to see Sophia watching them, a frown on her face and worry drawing her brows together. "Yes?"

"What's wrong?"

"Nothing I hope." Again the call went to voice mail.

Sophia scampered over to her, and Zoe drew the child to her side. Ginny stood near the edge of the window and peered out, careful to stay out of the line of fire. Zoe hit the lights and sent the room into darkness. Light from the kitchen filtered through the foyer and into the den.

She moved and kept Sophia right beside her. A thud sounded behind her coming from the kitchen. She whirled and Sophia gasped, but stayed right with her. Ginny stood there, the moonlight filtering through the blinds with enough light for Zoe to see her finger to her lips. In her other hand, she held her weapon.

Zoe pressed her lips together.

A knock on the door startled them all.

"Aaron," she breathed. Where was Joy? The tension curling in her belly formed into a hard ball. Ginny moved to the door.

"Zoe?" Aaron called. "What's going on? Are you all right?"

Ginny opened the door and pulled him inside and shut and relocked the door. "Someone's outside. Did you see Joy?"

His frown deepened. "No."

Her lips tightened and Zoe's fear level doubled. "She could be hurt," Zoe said. "I tried to call you but you didn't answer."

He checked his phone and grimaced. "It's on silent." He flipped the button. "Want me to check on Joy?"

Ginny paced from the window to the door. "She could have caught the guy," Ginny said. She checked her radio then looked at Aaron. "Joy, come in, are you there?" Zoe noted that she didn't use the police lingo. The two women were friends, coworkers. And Ginny was worried. Zoe's fear surged and she sent up a silent prayer. She had to.

"Joy didn't call for backup," Ginny said, hesitating. She was clearly torn between staying with Zoe and Sophia and going outside to find her fellow officer. "I'm calling for backup," she said, dialing her phone. Zoe thought she heard Lance's voice saying he was on the way.

"Go find her," Zoe said.

"Go," Aaron echoed. "I'll stay here with Zoe and Sophia."

"I can't," Ginny whispered. "I can't leave you." She paced to the door then the window. "The floodlights are on. Someone tripped them."

"I'll check the back of the house," Aaron said. He disappeared through the foyer into the main area, bypassed the kitchen and went to the back door off the living room. Zoe's gaze darted between Aaron and Ginny.

She moved a few steps into the den and waited while he peered out. She heard his gasp. "What is it?"

"Joy. She's on the ground and she's not moving." He glanced back. "Stay here."

"Aaron, no!" Ginny and Zoe said in unison. But they were speaking to his back.

Aaron stepped onto the porch. He back itched like someone had painted a big target on it, but he assured himself that the person was after Zoe and Sophia, not him. The pep talk didn't help, but it didn't stop him, either. It *did* help to hear the sirens approaching. He knelt beside the still deputy and felt for a pulse. It pounded beneath his fingers and he drew in a breath of relief.

"Is she all right?" Zoe called from the porch.

"She's alive. Get back inside." His fingers ran over the back of her head and encountered a large lump. He didn't want to take a chance on moving her in case she had a neck injury.

He heard a rustle to his left and spun to see a shadow move into the few trees at the edge of the property. "Hey! Tell Ginny he's out here!"

Aaron bolted after the now fleeing figure. No way was he letting this guy get away. He had a chance to end this now. He heard Ginny and Zoe call his name, but the adrenaline rushing through him lent speed to his feet and heightened his senses. His blood pounded in his veins. He heard the moment the person moved from the lawn onto the pavement. With Zoe's house right in the center of town, there were only a few sporadic trees and he was now past them, his eyes on the figure he refused to lose. The figure was smaller than Aaron, but quick as lightning. He noted the stares of the people he passed, but ignored them. He just prayed the guy didn't pull his weapon and start shooting.

He heard running feet behind him and figured it was Ginny. Either backup had arrived or she felt like she could leave Zoe and Sophia alone long enough to help in the chase. Or the person he was after had brought help. No time to rethink his decision to go after the man.

The fleeing man whipped around into the open and then disappeared around the side of the small café. People on the street turned to stare, but Aaron sped past them. He figured the man was heading for the road that ran behind the next strip of stores. He gritted his teeth, put on a burst of speed and closed the gap.

His fingers grazed the man's collar, then he hooked a finger on the inside. Joy's attacker went down, and Aaron tumbled after him. They both hit hard and the air left Aaron's lungs with a whoosh. Slamming into the asphalt at full speed *hurt*.

Stunned, Aaron lay there for a brief second that he couldn't afford. Finally, with a pained grunt, he heaved himself to his feet and moved toward the man who'd caused them all so much trouble. The attacker saw him coming and pushed himself to his knees. Aaron moved faster and shoved him back to the cement then reached over to grab his mask.

The man rolled to his back, and his fist shot

out to catch Aaron in the stomach. Aaron lost the rest of his breath when he went down to his knees, but the mask came off. Their eyes met.

"Freeze! Police!" Ginny's voice rang out.

A gun appeared in the man's hand, pulled from somewhere behind his back. He shoved it at Aaron who threw himself to the side. A shot rang out. The gawkers on the street screamed and dove for cover. The man backed away then turned and ran. Ginny didn't return fire, and Aaron saw why. An elderly couple stood frozen with fear right in the line of fire watching the fleeing criminal. Aaron rolled to his feet, ignoring his aches and pains and stumbled after the man. Just in time to see him jump into a black sedan and roar away.

Zoe's nerves had stretched to the breaking point by the time Aaron came limping up the back porch. Ginny walked behind him throwing glances over her shoulder every few seconds. Paramedics were lifting Joy onto the stretcher. Sophia hovered at Zoe's side. "Stay here, honey," Zoe told her.

"But Mom—"

"Stay here. You'll be able to see me. Don't move."

Zoe ran down to him and met him halfway across the back lawn. "Are you all right?"

"Yes. I'm fine. You shouldn't have come out of the house. It's possible he could circle back."

She grabbed his arm and he winced. "He's gone for now. And you're not fine, you're hurt."

"Just bruised. I landed pretty hard when I tried to recreate my days of Friday night football."

Zoe trotted along beside him. "I heard a gunshot."

"Yes, but he missed."

She led him up the steps and into the house. Sophia stood just inside the door where Zoe left her. Her tight face of concern met them. "Are you okay, Doctor Aaron?"

"I'll be just fine, sweetie."

Sophia didn't look convinced. "Did you get shot?"

"No, sweetheart, I fell."

Zoe led him to the kitchen table and he sank into the nearest chair. She pulled another chair around for him to prop his leg on. "He got away, didn't he?" she asked.

"Unfortunately," Aaron said. "Is Joy going to be okay?"

"Yes, Ginny waited for the paramedics to check her then took off after you. He must have caught her by surprise and hit her pretty hard with something."

"Probably the gun he had with him," Aaron murmured.

Zoe shuddered. "I'm so sorry about all of this."

"It's what they do, Zoe," Aaron murmured. "No apology necessary."

"But it's not what you do. You shouldn't be chasing intruders across my backyard."

He reached out and cupped her cheek. "It's okay, Zoe. I want to be here for you. We all do."

She knew that, but she still didn't want them to be in danger because of her. Sophia hovered. "Will you get Doctor Aaron a glass of water, hon?"

Sophia jumped into action. She poured him a glass of water and handed it to him. He chugged it. "Thanks, Sophia."

"You want another one?"

"Sure."

Once he had it refilled, Zoe drew Sophia next to her side. "Tell me everything." She hated for Sophia to have to hear it, but the child needed to understand the danger involved.

"Actually," Lance said, coming into the kitchen from the living area, "tell *us* everything." Deputy Walter Haywood followed, his notebook out, pen ready. Once Aaron finished relaying the events to Walter and Lance's satisfaction, he rubbed his eyes. Zoe could see his weariness wearing on him. Lance looked tired, as well. "You got a pretty good look at this guy?" Lance asked.

"Yeah, I managed to get his mask off and could describe him or pick him out of a lineup. Ginny may have seen him, too."

Lance nodded. "Come down to the station and work with Edie as soon as you can."

"Edie?" Zoe asked.

"Edie Travers," Walter said. "She's a local artist who's trained as a sketch artist. She mostly works with the Nashville Police Department, but offers her services to Wrangler's Corner when it's needed. Which, thankfully, isn't often."

"I can do that," Aaron said. "Tell her to call me with a time."

"Good. I'll see if she can meet with you first thing in the morning," Walter said.

Aaron nodded. "Fine."

"And while you're doing that," Lance said, "Parker and I are going to head to Knoxville to see if we can talk to the Bishop family." He looked at Zoe. "Walter will be watching you while Ginny stays with Sophia."

"Okay," Zoe said. "Let us know what you find out?"

"Of course."

"How is Joy? Have you heard anything? Is she going to be all right?" Zoe asked.

"Ginny's with her." He glanced at his phone. "She said she would text me when she knew something, but before they took off to the hospital, the paramedic said he thought she'd just had a hard knock to the head. A possible concussion, but he seemed to think she should be just fine."

Relief swept over her. "I hope so."

"All right, you guys get to your dinner, and I'll be in touch. Parker's going to be here for a while then I'll take over around one in the morning. That way we can both get some rest before we have to leave for Knoxville."

Lance left, and Zoe walked into the kitchen to pull the chicken from the oven. She grimaced and glanced up at Aaron who'd followed her. "It's a little over done, but it's edible."

"I'm sure it's amazing."

"If you'll tell Parker and Sophia it's ready, I'll get it on the table."

Aaron let his eyes linger on hers. She looked away to focus on the food. He sighed and walked to the den where Sophia played a game on the laptop and Parker rotated between the windows, pushing the curtains aside to peer out. "You guys ready to eat?"

Sophia popped up from the chair. "I am. I'm starving."

Aaron held out a hand and she grasped his fingers. The walls around his heart cracked even further and he knew he was in trouble. He'd always loved children and animals, took joy in and wanted to protect their innocence, unconditional love and loyalty. Probably why he'd fallen so hard for the single mother who'd run off with her ex-husband. And now he was doing it again. He grunted at his foolishness. He could fight it. Probably should. Over the past few days, this duo had done serious damage to the walls he'd erected around his heart.

They walked into the kitchen, and Sophia pulled him over to the chair next to hers. He smiled and settled himself at the table. Parker looked uneasy. "I'll just nibble while I keep tabs on the windows. I don't want to let my guard down."

Zoe nodded. "Of course. Feel free to fix a plate and take it into the den."

Parker did and when he vanished into the next room, Aaron looked at Zoe on one side of him and Sophia on the other. He swallowed hard. They could be a family. A small unit doing life together. He found he wasn't opposed to the idea and that set his self-protective alarm bells clanging. Hadn't he just been thinking he needed to repair the damage to the walls he'd put up?

She wasn't going to be here long. She was leaving and she was taking Sophia with her. Not necessarily because of another man, but the end result would be the same. He'd be alone with his shattered heart once again.

"Aaron?"

He blinked. "Oh, sorry, just thinking."

"About?"

He cleared his throat. "Ah..." His phone rang, rescuing him from having to come up with an answer. He pulled the phone from the clip. "Excuse me, it's Lance. I need to take it."

"Of course," Zoe said.

"Hello?"

"Aaron, Edie's in Knoxville for the day, but said she could fit you in after we talk to the Bishops. How do you feel about riding with us in the morning?"

He mentally ran through the list of things he needed to do in the morning. "That's fine. I'll let Nate know what's going on. If he's not planning to be there, I can shut the office for the day." He never closed except for the weekends and emergencies. He figured this qualified.

"Good. Be ready around eight. I'll pick you up."

"I'll be ready."

"Oh, and interestingly enough, Amber had some success in finding out where Zoe spent that year she went off grid."

"Really? Where?" He didn't look at her, afraid she'd pick up on the fact that she was the topic of conversation.

"She wouldn't say. Just said it wasn't anything illegal and if Zoe wanted us to know, she'd tell us."

Aaron rubbed his chin. "Huh. Okay then. Good to know."

"She said she ran into a dead end on Zoe's brother, though."

"Okay. Thanks." He hung up and saw Zoe and Sophia watching him. "I'll be riding to Knoxville in the morning with Lance and Parker." He explained the reason why.

She nodded. "I hope it helps catch this person."

"I do, too." He cleared his throat. "Would you like for me to say the blessing?" She frowned and he paused in the act of bowing his head. "What is it?"

Her frown slipped into a forced smile. "Nothing. Of course you can say the blessing."

"My mom's mad at God," Sophia whispered.

Zoe flinched. "Soph…"

Sophia shrugged. "Well, aren't you?"

Zoe's face reddened. "I'm not mad at God," she said. "I might be a bit frustrated with Him, but I'm not mad."

"You're not speaking to Him. I think that means mad."

At Zoe's ferocious frown, Sophia poked her lip out. Her gaze flicked to her mother, to Aaron then back to her mom. "Sorry," she muttered. "Was that 'crossing the line'?"

"By several feet."

Sophia ducked her head. "I'm sorry."

Aaron reached under the table and snagged the girl's fingers and squeezed. She looked up at him. At Zoe's sigh, Aaron said, "I think she'll forgive you."

Zoe gave a humorless chuckle. "All is forgiven. Now pray so we can eat." Her lips softened. "Maybe it's time I started saying grace again anyway. Even in the midst of all this craziness, there's quite a bit to be thankful for." Her eyes lingered on his and then slid to Sophia.

Aaron bowed his head and Sophia left her small hand in his. "Lord, we ask that you bless this food. We pray that you touch Joy with healing. Please protect Zoe and Sophia and those who are trying to catch the person after them. Thank you so much for the protection you've already placed around them. Amen."

"Amen," Sophia echoed.

Aaron thought he heard a whispered "Amen" from Zoe, as well.

He looked at the two females sitting on either side of him. He realized he wouldn't be building any walls around his heart. It was too late. He had fallen fast and hard. Now he added a silent prayer just between him and God. *Please don't let anything happen to them, and I'd really appreciate it if you'd convince Zoe to stay in Wrangler's Corner. But if for some reason this isn't to be, show me how to pick up the pieces and move on after they're gone.*

TWELVE

Within the cover of the enclosed garage, Zoe zipped Sophia's coat then watched her get into the backseat of the police cruiser. Ginny sat at the wheel speaking into the phone. "Yes, that's fine. It's not a problem, I've got it covered. Bye." She hung up with a frown.

"Problem?" Zoe asked.

"No, not really. Just something concerning my sister. I'll deal with it later."

"Anything I can do to help?"

"No." She offered Zoe a confident smile. "Have a good day."

"I will. You, too."

Zoe shut the door, thought two seconds then opened it before Ginny could back the car out. Sophia looked up. "Did you forget something?"

"Come on back inside, hon. You're not going to school today." She just couldn't send her. She looked at Ginny. "I'm sorry. It's not safe. Especially not after last night. I just don't want to let her out of my sight."

"But I want to go," Sophia protested. "And I'm with Deputy Ginny. I'll be fine."

Still Zoe stood frozen with indecision raging.

"I understand your fear," Ginny said. "But really it might be more safe for her to be at school than here, though."

"What do you mean?"

"At the school, there's the school resource officer as well as a plainclothes officer at each entrance of the building. After what happened last night, Clay called in a few of his buddies from when he was with the Nashville Police Department. There are some plainclothes watching your house, as well."

"Oh." She drew in a deep breath. "Well, in that case…"

"She'll be fine, I promise."

Still Zoe hesitated. "Come on, Mom, I'm going to be late. Please?"

"All right," she said. "With all that security, I guess you're right."

"Yes!" Sophia pumped her fist in the air, and Zoe stepped back. Ginny gave a small salute and Zoe pressed the button to lift the garage door.

She watched them leave then pressed the

button once more to lower the door. Back inside, she paced from window to window, peering out and wondering where those plain-clothes officers were. Then again, if they were good at their job, she wouldn't be able to see them, right?

A knock on the door stiffened her spine. Deputy Haywood pulled his weapon and moved from the kitchen barstool to the door to look out. He relaxed a fraction and holstered his gun. "It's Sabrina's grandmother, Yvonne Mayfield, from across the street. She runs the bed-and-breakfast."

"Of course. Please, let her in."

Walter opened the door and the woman stepped inside. In her hands she held a basket covered with a red-and-white checkered cloth. "Hello."

"Hi there. I know we haven't been properly introduced, but Clay mentioned your troubles and I wanted to stop by and see if you needed anything. I'm Yvonne Mayfield, but you can just call me Granny May."

"Well, thank you, Granny May. I'm Zoe. Won't you come in and have a seat?"

"No, I've got to get back." She handed Zoe the basket. "Just enjoy those and get the basket back to me anytime."

Zoe lifted the edge of the cloth and cinnamon wafted up to her. "These smell yummy."

"Oh, they're good all right." The wizened woman smiled revealing a full set of white dentures. She had to be in her eighties, but she stood ramrod straight, shoulders thrown back and head held high. "Well, you stay safe, young lady. And I'll be watching out for you, too."

Zoe felt a knot form in her throat. Small-town life. She could grow to love it. "Thank you. And congratulations on the birth of your great-grandchild."

Her face glowed. "It's definitely exciting." She glanced over her shoulder. "Gotta run now. You take care."

Zoe thanked her again and the deputy opened the door for her. When he turned back, his eyes were on the basket.

Zoe held it out to him and he grinned, reached in and promptly wolfed down two of the cookies.

"I take it you're familiar with Granny May's cooking?"

"Yes, ma'am. Can't beat it."

Zoe took one of the cookies and let him carry the basket into the kitchen. She wondered if there would be any left if she wanted another.

Wrangler's Corner. A small town with a

sweet woman who didn't let a little trouble keep her away from welcoming a stranger. A deputy's office that was going all out to keep her and her daughter safe. And a man named Aaron Starke who obviously wanted her and Sophia to stay in town for the duration, but was willing to put his own wants on the back burner if it meant keeping her safe.

She walked into the kitchen to find Walter finishing off one more cookie. He reddened. "You caught me."

She laughed. "It's fine. My daughter has diabetes so I have to monitor her sugar intake very carefully. Go ahead and eat them, just save her one."

He smiled. "I won't argue with you."

"I figured." Yes, she could get used to a place like Wrangler's Corner. She might be tempted to make the town her permanent home if she could just figure out—and stop—who wanted to bury her in the local cemetery.

THIRTEEN

The drive to Knoxville passed in a blur and soon Aaron found himself staring up at a large house in one of the best neighborhoods in the city. "Nice," he said.

"Yeah." Lance put the car in Park. A local police cruiser sat at the curb across the street and Lance nodded. "Good. They're here. I called before we left Wrangler's Corner and asked that someone monitor the house and let me know if anyone left. So far, everyone must still be here."

Walter reported in, and Aaron thought about Zoe sitting at home waiting for news. He hoped they'd have some to give her soon enough. Lance stepped out of the vehicle, and Aaron shivered when the cold air blasted him. "I'm going to just hang here, is that all right?"

Lance nodded. "That's fine." He paused. "Actually, why don't you go with us?"

"Why?"

"You got a look at the intruder last night. Let's see if you recognize Gregory Bishop."

Good point. "All right." Aaron got out of the car and Lance nodded Parker to go first. Parker led the way followed by Lance and Aaron.

"Stand off to the side," Lance said. "If it's him and he recognizes you then there could be trouble. I don't want him to see you until the last minute."

"Right." Aaron stood where directed. Parker knocked and then stepped back and to the other side. Just in case someone decided to shoot through the door? Possibly.

But no bullets came through the door. Instead, it swung open and a woman in her late twenties with blue eyes and auburn hair stood in the entryway. "Yes?"

Lance flashed his badge as did Parker. "We're deputies working a case. We're also friends of your sister-in-law, Zoe Collier."

"Zoe?" Surprise lit the woman's eyes. "Is she all right? And Sophia?"

"Yes, they're both fine for now."

"Oh, good." She placed a hand over her chest. "You scared me."

"Do you mind if we come in and ask you a few questions?"

The request seemed to fluster her for a moment but she stepped back and let them in. She didn't question Aaron's presence, and he didn't offer her an ID or explanation.

She led them into the family room and gestured for them to take a seat on the large leather sofa. "You said Zoe and Sophia are all right."

"Yes, ma'am. Is your husband home?"

"Yes, he's in the garage. We just got back from vacation last night and he's cleaning out the car."

"Vacation? Where did you go?"

"Just to Radnor Lake. We have a house there."

"I see." Aaron figured Lance was making notes to check that out. "Do you mind asking your husband to come in here? It'll save me the trouble of having to ask the same questions twice."

A small frown drew her brows together, but she simply shrugged. "Of course." She stood and Parker followed her. Aaron figured he wasn't taking a chance she'd go after a weapon. Lance's phone beeped while the two were gone. He looked at it then muttered something under his breath.

"What was that?" Aaron asked.

"Sorry. Clay texted. He just got the autopsy result for Pete, the guy you shot."

"Yeah." *The guy you shot*. Aaron didn't think he'd ever get used to hearing those words.

"Looks like he didn't die from your gunshot wounds."

Aaron blinked. "He didn't?"

"No. He was suffocated."

Zoe checked the clock and frowned. Sophia should have been home by now. She thought about giving Ginny a few more minutes, but then decided she might as well check in now. She dialed the number and waited. When it went to voice mail, she hung up and tried again. Anxiety kicked in. She dialed Clay's number. "Hello?"

She could hear the baby crying in the background. "I'm so sorry to bother you."

"Zoe? It's no bother. What can I do for you?"

"Sophia was supposed to be home about fifteen minutes ago. I tried Ginny's number, but she didn't answer. I know it's silly to panic because of a fifteen-minute delay, but I was wondering if you could get in touch with Ginny and just see where they are."

"Of course. Stay by your phone and I'll call you right back."

"Thank you." She hung up and fought the

urge to crumple to the floor and wail. Somehow, she knew something was dreadfully wrong. *Please, God, let Sophia and Ginny be all right.*

Her phone buzzed. "Clay?"

"Actually, this is your father-in-law, Zoe. How are you doing?"

"Alexander? I-I'm fine. How are you? How did you get this number?"

"Well, I wasn't exactly sure it was you, just hopeful. Nina said she'd had someone call and hang up from a number she didn't recognize. The more I thought about it, the more I thought it might be you. It's good to hear your voice, sweetheart."

She used a shaky hand to shove a lock of hair behind her ear. "Yours, too, Alexander."

"How's Sophia?"

"She's fine."

"Well, I...ah...was wondering if you'd be willing to meet me and have coffee somewhere. I have some things I'd like to talk to you about."

"Like what?" She glanced at the clock. Why hadn't Clay called her back yet?

"Like the fact that you just disappeared with Sophia. I miss her, Zoe. I want her home."

Zoe let out a little sigh. "I know, Alexander.

That's what I want, too, but someone tried to kidnap her. And then someone tried to run me off the road. The police said they couldn't do anything so I had to run. And since we've been here, you wouldn't believe what's happened."

"Then come home where I can protect you. Go pack your bags and I can come get you and Sophia."

She closed her eyes and searched her mind for the right words. He just didn't get it. "I've got help and I've got protection right now. Coming back to Knoxville wouldn't be the safest thing for us to do right now."

"Zoe—"

Her phone buzzed. She looked at the screen then pressed the phone back to her ear. "I've got to take this call, Alexander. I'll talk to you later."

"Zoe—"

Another beep from Clay. The last one before the call would go to voice mail. She switched lines. "Clay?"

"Zoe, I can't reach Ginny, either." His grim tone made her stiffen. "Sophia never showed up to school," he said.

She gasped. "What? Why didn't the school call me?"

"They said a woman called claiming to be

you and said Sophia was sick and would be staying home today."

"No I didn't! Who? Who called?"

"I don't know. I've requested phone records from the school, but it's going to take a little bit to get them. I'm also cross-checking the records against Nina's and Gregory's numbers."

"How long is a little bit? What about Sophia?" Tears threatened, but she had to hold it together.

"I've got every available deputy searching for her and Ginny. I've tried pinging her phone, but it's not registered as being on. But I'm also checking her phone records and texts as we speak."

"What do I do? How can I help? Where is she, Clay?"

"I don't know, Zoe, but don't panic. We'll find her. Stay by the phone, I'll be in touch."

He hung up and Zoe sank onto the couch, her legs no longer having the strength to support her. She buried her face in her hands and tried to gather her thoughts. Sophia, her child, her baby, was missing and she didn't know who had her. Zoe dropped to her knees. "Please, God, take care of her and bring her and Ginny back safely."

FOURTEEN

Aaron sat back, his breath leaving his lungs with a whoosh. "Suffocated? Is he sure?"

"He's sure."

"But how? Why? Who?"

"All good questions." Footsteps interrupted the conversation. Aaron looked up to see Nina enter the living area followed by a man in his early thirties. He looked tanned in spite of the time of year. He also looked unfamiliar. This wasn't the man he'd tackled. He looked at Lance and gave a subtle shake of his head. Gregory wasn't the man he'd chased last night.

Lance pursed his lips and took a seat. The Bishops did, as well. "What's this all about?" Gregory asked.

"It's about your sister-in-law, Zoe Collier."

Gregory frowned. "What about her?"

Lance launched into the explanation of the attempts on her life and the results of his investigation. "It appears that one of the men hired to kidnap or kill—we haven't determined exactly which one they were attempting—received a phone call from this number." He read the number.

Gregory rocked back, and Nina gasped. "What?"

"That's your home number, right?" Lance asked.

"Well, yes, but—"

Their surprise was real. Aaron grimaced. Would they never get to the bottom of this?

He let his gaze wander the room once again. He noticed the collage of horse pictures on the far wall and figured they portrayed the horse Trevor and Zoe had owned. He stood and began looking at each picture, wondering if Zoe or Sophia were in any of them. He found them in several. They looked happy enough. Trevor was a handsome man. Sophia looked a bit like him. In the last picture, Aaron stopped and looked closer. The man petting the neck of the horse looked familiar.

"I don't believe it," Nina said. "Gregory?"

Gregory spread his hands. "When was the call made?"

Lance told him, and Gregory shook his

head. "That's impossible. There's been no one here."

"Did you have a house sitter? A pet sitter? Anyone that might have come in to put your mail on the counter?"

"No. We don't have any pets, and we stopped the mail service until tomorrow. I'm telling you, there's no way someone managed to get in our house without setting off the security alarm, much less use our phone."

Lance rubbed his head. "All right, then is there anyone else who has a key to your house, the code to your alarm, who might have decided to come in for any reason without your knowledge?"

"No, no keys out there, but..." Nina bit her lip.

"But what?" Parker asked.

She sighed. "We have a garage code. There are several people who have it and can get in the house that way."

Lance ripped a sheet of paper from his notebook. "Write down their names, will you?"

She took the paper and pen from him and began her list. While she wrote, Lance cleared his throat. "I know that this is a rather delicate subject, but we've done some investigating into your backgrounds. We've noticed you're having some financial issues."

Nina's head snapped up. "Investigating *us*?"

"Yes. Everything points to you or your husband being behind everything that's happened to Zoe and Sophia over the past few weeks. We had to run down every lead."

Her face turned a bright red and she stood, dropping the paper on the floor. "That's ridiculous. What leads? How would we benefit from anything happening to Zoe?"

"You get Sophia if she dies," Lance said without raising his voice or changing his expression.

Nina sank back into her seat and looked at her husband. "Yes. That's true, but she doesn't come with any money."

"Thunderbolt," Gregory said.

Lance nodded. "And with Sophia, you get Thunderbolt whose worth is estimated at around two hundred fifty thousand dollars. That would go a long way toward paying off some of those creditors you're going to have knocking on your door soon."

"Why do you think we've been up at the lake house this time of year?" Nina demanded. "We're getting it ready to put on the market to sell."

Lance leaned back and Gregory stood to pace while Aaron watched him. There was something in his expression, something he wasn't saying. "What is it?" Lance asked him.

Gregory stopped midpace. "I don't know. Nothing. I'm just trying to think."

"About?"

"Nothing."

"Something. What is it?"

Gregory spread his hands in a beseeching gesture. "Look, I made some bad investments. My father-in-law talked me into investing in several companies owned by a friend of his. A little over two years ago, the bottom dropped out. I managed to get out before I lost everything. My father-in-law hasn't been so fortunate. I warned him. I told him I thought he needed to sell, that something was wrong with the way the stock was dropping, but he insisted on hanging in there. We've been helping him as much as we can, but we're about at the end of our resources."

"This is all his fault," Nina said. "And yours," she directed to Gregory. "If you hadn't listened to him, we would be fine."

"We're still fine," Gregory snapped. "As soon as the lake house sells, everything will be okay again. It's just going to take some time."

"Time that we don't really have."

"Yes, we do. We'll get through this." He moved to sit beside his wife and took her hand. She sniffed and looked away, but left her hand in her husband's. He looked at Lance, then Aaron. "And we don't need to kill my sister-in-law to do it. You're looking at the wrong people."

Lance nodded and rubbed his head. "One last question. Why would you call the men at the ranch?"

"What men?"

"The men who were after Sophia and Zoe. The men who held a law enforcement officer and three innocent people hostage," Lance said.

Gregory's eyes widened, then he frowned. "I don't know what you're talking about. I just told you that we weren't here. There was no one *in this house* to make any calls *from this house*. You must be mistaken."

Lance stayed silent for a moment. When he didn't seem to have anything else to say, Aaron tapped the picture that held the familiar figure. "Who's this guy with the horse?"

With a perturbed look at Lance, Gregory turned his attention to Aaron and walked over to squint at the picture. "Oh, that's Brian Cartee. He's Thunderbolt's jockey. Why?"

Before Aaron had a chance to answer,

Lance's phone buzzed. He glanced at the screen. "Excuse me, I need to take this. It's Clay calling, hopefully with an update." He stood and walked into the foyer. Aaron followed him with every intention of eavesdropping. Plus, he'd just placed the man in the picture.

"Missing?" He heard Lance suck in a deep breath. "All right. Ginny, too? Yeah. Yeah. I'll tell him."

When he turned around, Aaron didn't like the expression in Lance's eyes. "Tell me."

"Someone attacked Ginny's car. There are bullet holes in the side of the car and blood on the ground. She and Sophia are missing."

Aaron felt light-headed for a moment. "Missing? Blood?"

"I'm asking for help from the FBI. We don't have the resources they do and I don't want to take any chances on this not ending well."

"We need to get back now."

"Yes."

"But first. That man in the picture on the Bishops' mantel? Brian Cartee? He's the jockey for Sophia's horse. I've seen him before."

"Where?"

"When I tackled him outside of Zoe's

house. He's the one who attacked Joy and the one who ran from me."

Lance sucked in a deep breath. "This just keeps getting more and more interesting. We need to let Zoe know."

"I'll be in the car. I'm calling her to fill her in and let her know we're on the way." He pulled his phone from his pocket and hit her speed-dial number.

Zoe was still in a state of numbed shock when the three men walked into the house five hours later. She stood when they stepped into the den. "Brian? Brian Cartee is the man who attacked Joy? Who managed to over-power Ginny and grab Sophia? And where is all the protection she said was in place?"

Lance and Clay exchanged glances. "Protection? What are you talking about? You mean about Parker and Walter?"

"No, she said Clay had called some friends from Nashville and they were watching the school and the house and—" At Clay's blank look, she snapped her lips together. "She lied. Why would she lie?" She shuddered and bit back a sob. "She's a part of it."

Clay pulled his phone. "I've got some calls to make." He looked at Zoe. "I'm sorry. Ginny's new, but she came with good references, and I've never had any reason to believe she'd do something like this. I'm going to figure out what's going on right now." He paused. "But before I do, why would Brian be in Nina and Gregory's house?"

She rubbed her head. "I don't know. I don't know anything. None of this makes any sense."

"Let's think about this. Why would Brian come after you or Sophia now? What does he gain if you're dead and Sophia in his possession?"

"Nothing! That's what I'm saying. If I die, everything goes to Nina and Gregory. Including Sophia."

"What if they've worked a deal with him?" Aaron said. "You said he wanted the horse. How bad do Nina and Gregory want Sophia? You said Nina wanted the two of you to come live with her?"

"Well, yes, but she wouldn't do this." She shook her head. "No, something's not adding up. We're missing something else."

"Does Brian have access to Nina and Gregory's house?"

She rubbed her forehead. "No, not that I know of. He and Trevor were really close, but Gregory is a bit of a snob. He doesn't associate with people he considers not on his level.

So to speak." She grimaced. "In other words, no. There's no reason Brian would have been in their house."

"Unless he broke in," Aaron said.

Zoe shook her head. "He would have set the alarm off."

"Not if someone gave him the code," Lance said.

"Which Gregory would do if Brian was doing his dirty work."

"Maybe," Aaron said and shrugged. "It's all speculation."

Clay pursed his lips. "All right. You think some more on it. I've got a BOLO out on Brian. He wasn't home when officers went by his house earlier. They stopped by the barn and there was no sign of him there, either." He exchanged a look with Lance. "Which could mean he's somewhere close by. Be sure to keep your eyes open."

"Of course."

"Now about—"

Zoe tuned them out as her thoughts went to Sophia. She knew Brian. Trusted him. Would feel safe with him. Would he hurt her? Scare her? Know to give her her medicine? Sophia kept an emergency insulin kit in her backpack. She stopped and spun toward the men. "Did Sophia have her backpack with her?"

Clay pulled the phone from his ear. "If she had it when she left the house, she—or who-ever has her—probably has it with her. The car was cleaned out."

A slight tug of relief found its way into her shattered mother's heart. She continued to pace and pray while Clay made his calls and Lance and Aaron discussed the incident.

Incident. Her daughter's kidnapping was an incident. The thought made her want to throw up. How could this have happened? She'd been so careful. Her thoughts continued to circle that loop until she couldn't get past it. "I did everything you said," she whispered. Lance and Aaron turned toward her. The pain in Aaron's eyes fueled her own. "How could this happen? How could Brian just take her away from Ginny? How could Ginny let his happen?" Her voice rose with each word and she couldn't seem to stop the sweeping anger mixed with hysteria and downright terror. "I. Did. *Everything*. You. Said!"

Aaron caught her by the forearms. She re-sisted for a brief moment then let him pull her against his chest. His heart thumped beneath her cheek as she saturated his shirt with her tears. He said nothing, just held her. With each sob, she mentally ordered herself to stop, to get control, but the thought of never seeing her child again set off more spasms of pain and grief. Finally, she drew in a deep breath and pulled away from the comfort of his embrace. He let her go, but led her into the den area. She noticed Clay and Lance had made themselves scarce. Aaron pressed a tissue into her hand and she dropped onto the couch.

"This probably isn't the best time to ask, but maybe talking about something else will help." He lowered himself beside her.

She eyed him warily. "Okay."

"I've been thinking. You said something the other day that I've been meaning to ask you about and haven't gotten around to it."

Oh. That. She figured she knew what was coming.

"Will you tell me about the drug problem you mentioned?"

Yep, she was right. Oh, boy. She'd known he would address it at some point, but had hoped to avoid that conversation a bit longer. "Why do you want to know?"

He frowned. "Because if Brian is behind this—and it looks like he is—he could be working with someone. It already looks like Ginny's involved. Three men were hired to try and kidnap Sophia. We need to make sure no one else is in this loop. So can you think of anyone who has a past with drugs and might have found his or her way into your present for some kind of revenge? Someone who would be willing to take money to get rid of you?"

She pressed her fingertips to her burning eyes. "It was such a long time ago. I don't think this is related to that."

"It might not be, but Clay needs to address every possibility. And if you used to hang out with—" He paused and grimaced.

"Junkies?"

"Well, yes, but I was trying to find a better way to say it."

"There's not a better way. We were rich kids, but we were still addicts." She groaned and shook her head. "It was stupid. I was stupid. My dad went to prison when I was thirteen. Three years later he was home and wanting to make his marriage work. My mother would have none of it. She wanted him out of the house and he refused to go."

"So why didn't your mother leave?"

"She did eventually. But when everything started happening—when my father was finally released from prison and home—she had nowhere to go. She had no real friends. She was too ashamed to go to the church for help. But she finally had a friend say she could move in with her for a short time."

"She left you with your father?"

Zoe sighed. "Yes. And I get it now. My mother was depressed, desperate and very, very angry." She shrugged. "My dad finally consented to the divorce, but still refused to move out. The fighting was just—" she spread her hands and shuddered "—awful, to say the least. I was looking for an escape. I found that in painting. And then drugs. I knew I shouldn't have, but one night, the fighting was just too much. My father was bitter about his prison time. My mother was packing her suitcase and screaming at the top of her lungs about how it was a shame he didn't even have the decency to leave her and me in peace and go find a place of his own, he yelled back that he didn't have a job or any money so how was he supposed to make that happen…" She took a deep breath and brushed away a stray tear. "I went over to my boyfriend's house and he gave me what I'd been refusing for a while. I tried a little cocaine." She shrugged. "And it was…amazing. I was able to forget. Just for a bit, but it was such a *relief.* I didn't seem to have any ill effects from it so tried it again. And again. And soon it was all I thought about, all I craved. And before I realized what had happened, I was an addict." She gave a derisive laugh.

"I kept telling myself I could handle it, that it wasn't any big deal and that I'd quit when things got better at home. But…"

"But you couldn't quit."

"No, I couldn't. By the time life had settled down a bit, I was well and truly hooked."

"How'd you get clean?"

"Rehab. My parents paid for me to go, but refused to let me come home after I was out." She shrugged. "They'd moved on while I was away. Sold the house at this point and gone their separate ways. Neither of them wanted me back home. I can't say I completely blame them. I was horrible. I stole from them. I was defiant, disrespectful, mean-spirited." She gave a choked laugh. "That was the one thing they could agree on through the whole thing. I couldn't come back home."

"You were angry, lashing out at them while they were so focused on themselves."

"Oh, very much so. I knew what I was doing was wrong, but I wanted to hurt them. My father was a bigwig in the community, albeit a fallen one. I wanted him and all of his bigwig friends to know that he had a junkie for a daughter and that it was all his fault."

"You didn't blame your mother?"

"Not so much. She was part of the issue, but she was just weak. She couldn't deal with my father's theft, the trial, the conviction, the jail time. She just kind of checked out. But my father, he was a different story. He was livid to say the least."

"What *did* he say?"

"He told me I was no longer his child." She rubbed her eyes again and he took her hand. The fact that he hadn't run from her said a lot for his character. It encouraged her to finish the story. "So I went to my youth pastor at the church we attended sporadically. He managed to get me into a program sponsored by the church. And while I knew I needed help, I wasn't sure I could kick the habit. But the program was a good one with good people and excellent counselors." She shrugged. "I also got into a Bible study with a woman who seemed very taken with me. She really encouraged me, supported me…loved me." She took a deep breath. "And prayed for me. I eventually got out, went to college and left the drugs in the past. But it wasn't easy."

"I'm sure it wasn't. So that's where you were when you dropped off the radar for a year?"

She frowned. "Maybe. Why?"

"Clay did some checking up on you and said he couldn't find anything on you for about a year. Amber went to her sources and came back and said she knew where you'd been but it wasn't any of our business and if you wanted us to know, you'd tell us."

"Oh." She wasn't sure how she felt about the fact that Clay and Amber both had investigated her background, but guessed she understood why. She gave a slow nod then a small shrug. "But that's why I don't think it's anyone from my past. The old boyfriend who provided the drugs is also clean and is living and working in Haiti with some charitable organization."

"I'll get Lance to check on him anyway."

She nodded and stood. "His name's Matthew Holder. I'm going to my room. I need some time alone. Please come get me if you hear anything."

"Zoe—"

She held up a hand. "I just need some time, Aaron."

"Okay."

She could tell he didn't want her to leave, but she'd said enough and now she just wanted to be alone. To try and find her way out of the yawning black hole of pain and fear for her child. To process that Brian Cartee had been the one behind the attack on Joy and possibly had Sophia.

She shut the bedroom door behind her and sank onto the bed. Sophia's favorite stuffed animal had gotten caught between the pillow and the headboard. Zoe gripped it and clutched it to her chest. "Please, God, take care of my baby." She shed more tears into the soft fur and continued to pray.

Aaron felt helpless. He *was* helpless. And he hated the feeling. "We've got to find her, Lance. What are we missing? Zoe seems so sure it's not someone from her past."

Lance looked at his phone. "Well, Brian Cartee's dropped off the grid. We can't track him through his phone because he's not using it."

"Probably has a burner to communicate with whoever is behind this."

"Why do you think he's not the leader in this whole thing?" Lance asked.

"I don't really know. Call it just a gut feeling."

"Sometimes that's the best thing to go by."

"Yeah."

Lance glanced toward the back of the house. "Is she all right?"

Aaron blew out a sigh. "No, not really, but she will be. Eventually."

Clay stepped into the room, his face drawn, brows almost meeting at the bridge of his nose.

Aaron froze. "What is it? What else is wrong?"

"I just spoke to Amber."

"Amber?" Aaron raised a brow. "What's up with her?"

"Apparently she's got some pretty amazing contacts who owe her a ton of favors. Anyway, she just called to say that she did background checks on all of Zoe's family members. One person came back red-flagged."

"Wait a minute. You did background checks. Nothing showed up."

"Yes, I did one on Nina and Gregory when it looked like they had something to do with everything going on. The one person I didn't do was Alexander Collier."

"Zoe's father-in-law?"

"Yeah." Clay glanced at his phone again and shook his head.

"What showed up in Amber's search?"

"Collier's in debt up to his eyeballs, and his home is getting ready to be foreclosed on. He's been hanging on by his fingernails, but she said in about two more months, he's done."

"But it makes no sense for him to go after

Sophia and Zoe because she doesn't have the money to bail him out."

"Obviously he knows something we don't," Clay said.

"We have to tell her."

"Yeah."

"But how?"

The phone in her pocket buzzed, waking her from a restless doze. She blinked and rubbed her eyes then grabbed her phone praying the person on the other end had some news about Sophia. She glanced at the screen and winced. Her father-in-law. What was she going to tell him? That she'd failed? That she'd allowed his granddaughter to be taken? With another choked sob, she answered the call. "Hello?"

"I want you to listen to me very carefully."

Something in his tone made her sit up straight. "All right. What is it?"

"I want you to get out of the house without anyone seeing you."

She stilled. "What?"

"I know where Sophia is."

"What? Where? Is she okay? She has diabetes, Alexander, you know that. She needs her medicine. I need to get to her."

"She's safe and will stay that way for now as long as you follow my instructions."

Realization crashed over Zoe. "You," she whispered.

"Yes. Me."

Her whole body trembled. Her father-in-law had tried to kidnap his own grandchild and he'd hired men to kill Zoe. "Why?"

"Does it matter?"

"Of course it matters!"

"Shh. You don't want anyone to overhear you. Now look out of your window."

Zoe stood, her legs shaking and threatening to give way, but she locked her muscles and strode to the window. "Where's Ginny? Did you kill her?" She glanced out and found Alexander's tall form. He stood on the other side of the property fence, phone pressed to his ear, baseball cap pulled low over his eyes. No one would think anything about him being there. He looked like a neighbor hanging out in his backyard having a phone conversation with a friend. "I see you," she said.

"Good." He turned slightly and glanced in her direction. "And I see you. Ginny isn't important right now. What's important is that you follow my directions exactly."

"I will. Tell me."

"Don't hang up until I tell you that you can.

Get your keys and get out of the house without anyone noticing, walk down the street and get into the white Cadillac parked three doors down. I'll be waiting."

Her keys? Her purse was on the table next to the front door. "What if I can't?" she whispered.

"You'll find a way. Now come on. The longer you take the shorter Sophia's life span gets."

Zoe flinched. "Would you really hurt your own granddaughter?"

He scoffed. "You've never known me at all, have you?"

"Apparently not."

"Understand this, Zoe." His deadly tone had her full attention. "I will do whatever it takes to accomplish my goals and if that means Sophia dies, then so be it."

Zoe's breath left her. She turned from the window, hesitating as she considered her options. Then realized she had no options. At least for now. She looked at the pen on the small desk in the corner, picked it up and searched frantically for a piece of paper.

"What are you doing Zoe? What's taking so long?"

"I'm trying to figure out how to get out of

the house without anyone seeing me. It might take me a minute."

She scanned the desk again and looked back at the end table. If she crossed in front of the window, he would see her—and know she wasn't out of the room yet. She settled the pen against the wood of the desk and pressed. And the ink wouldn't flow. Stifling a sob of frustration, she pressed harder and gouged *Alexander has Sophia. White Cad—*

"Zoe…"

She didn't dare stay a moment longer. She dropped the pen, took a deep breath and left the bedroom and entered the hall. She could hear Alexander's breaths in her ear. He was nervous about this. And well he should be.

"Zoe?" The low warning in his voice made her shiver.

"I'm coming," she whispered.

She heard voices from the kitchen. Somehow she had to slip out the front door without them hearing or seeing. How? She drew closer and paused just outside the door as though planning to eavesdrop.

"…got Sophia," Clay said.

"Bottom line," Aaron said, "is that he wants Sophia alive and Zoe dead. Somehow it all comes back to money."

"So how are we going to break this to Zoe?" Aaron said.

She peered around the corner. Clay had his back to her, but Aaron was leaning against the counter with his arms crossed against his chest.

Zoe took a deep breath and waited, heart pounding. If one of them decided to leave the kitchen, he'd see her. She risked another glance.

Aaron dropped his hands and turned to get his glass from the counter. No time to hesitate. She slipped past the opening and into the foyer, grabbed her purse from the small table near the door and tucked it under her arm.

"Where are you, Zoe?" She could hear the anger in Alexander's voice, but couldn't take a chance on responding. Not yet. She twisted the knob of the front door and pulled it open wide enough to slip through then shut it slowly, careful to not make any noise.

She turned and took a deep breath. "I'm outside."

"Very good." The sudden confidence in his voice made her want to vomit. Was she wrong? Should she have signaled to Aaron or Lance somehow? No, she couldn't risk Alexander finding out and hurting Sophia. She remembered his tone when he said he would do anything to accomplish his goals. She had no doubt he'd hurt Sophia.

She looked up and down the street and spotted Yvonne Mayfield sweeping the front porch of the bed-and-breakfast. Zoe turned her gaze away, praying the woman would spot her, but doing nothing that would cause Alexander to suspect she was trying to get the woman's attention. Yvonne never looked up. Zoe bit the inside of her cheek. "Keep walking," Alexander said. "Come down the steps and turn left. Walk to the car and get in. Now."

Zoe did as ordered.

"Zoe? Is that you, hon?"

Zoe nearly stumbled, but didn't look back as she continued toward the white Cadillac. So Yvonne had seen her. If Alexander had the windows up, maybe he wouldn't realize the woman had called out to her. She got to the car and opened the passenger door. Her gaze went to the backseat but of course Sophia wasn't there. She stared at her father-in-law. "Where is she?"

"She's safe."

"How do I know that?"

He held up his cell phone and she stared at the picture on the screen. Sophia was sitting at a kitchen table drinking a glass of milk.

She knew that kitchen. Betrayal stabbed sharp and deep. "She's with Nina? Nina's behind this, too?"

"Get in and give me your cell phone."

Zoe resisted throwing a glance back toward her home and slid into the passenger seat. He snatched her phone from her fingers and powered it down. Her hands trembled and she clasped them together between her knees. Her child was safe for the moment, now it was up to her to figure out how to stay alive.

He pulled a roll of duct tape from beneath the seat and she cringed. "Alexander, please…"

His diamond-hard gaze cut into her. "Give me your hands."

She couldn't do it. "I'm not going to fight you," she said softly. "You have my child." She held his eyes, keeping hers steady. "As long as you have control of her, you have control of me."

He lifted a gun and pointed it at her head. "Give me your hands."

Her breath caught. Death stared her in the eye. She lifted her hands. He quickly taped them together, then shoved her back against the passenger door. Zoe felt the comforting weight of the small gun against her ankle. Unfortunately she had no way to get to it.

"Why do you want me dead? Why send those men to kill me and kidnap Sophia?"

"I need money, Zoe. A lot of money."

She stared at him and he pulled away from the curb. Fear clawed at her but she controlled it. She had to. Sophia was counting on her. "But I don't have a lot of money, Alexander. You know that as well as I do. You were there for the reading of the will. All I have is the horse and a little bit of life insurance money from Trevor—and I'll sign the horse over to you today. You can sell him for a quarter of a million."

"Two hundred fifty thousand is simply a drop in the bucket. And you're worth more than you think you are. Trevor took out a two-million-dollar life insurance policy on you a year before he died."

FIFTEEN

The knock on the door pulled Aaron from his thoughts on how to tell Zoe it looked like her father-in-law was behind the attempts on her life. Lance stood and followed him into the foyer. A peek out the window drained some of his tension. "It's Sabrina's grandmother." He opened the door. "Hi, Mrs. Mayfield."

"I just saw Zoe get into someone's car down the street. I called out to her, but she acted like she didn't hear me. With all the trouble she's been having I figured I'd better come see if everything was all right."

Aaron didn't answer. He bolted down the hall and found Zoe's bedroom door open. He glanced around the room and found it empty. Without bothering to investigate further, he spun on his heel. "Lance! She's not here." He raced back into the foyer.

Mrs. Mayfield shook her head. "Of course

she's not here. I just told you she got in a car and left with that man."

"What man?"

"Well, I don't know his name, but I did think to write down the license plate. It's a white Cadillac." She pulled a scrap of paper from her pocket and handed it over to Lance. "I would have been here faster, but I had to go inside and find a piece of paper or I would have forgotten the number between my place and here."

Lance kissed her cheek and pulled out his phone. He glanced at Aaron. "Try calling her on her cell."

Aaron nodded, but had a sinking feeling in his stomach. He dialed her number and as he was afraid it would, it went straight to voice mail. He hung up and found Lance writing something down.

Mrs. Mayfield still stood in the foyer wringing her hands. "I'll be praying."

"Yes, please," Aaron said. "Pray hard."

"Got it," Lance said.

"Got what?"

"The car is a rental out of Knoxville."

"Whose name is it in?"

"Jedidiah Mason."

Aaron flinched. "Jed. One of the guys who

held us all hostage at the ranch. He's the one who got away."

"No doubt hired by Alexander Collier. Fortunately, this company puts GPS trackers on all of their rentals." He pressed another button on his phone.

Aaron felt hope surge. Finally, it was time to bring this to an end. He just prayed they found Zoe before it was too late.

Zoe was stunned, rocked to her very core as his words echoed over and over in her mind. "Two-million-dollar life insurance policy?" Surely she'd heard wrong. "That's crazy."

"Yes. And I need that two million dollars. Yesterday."

"Why?" she whispered. "Trevor never said a word. I never found any paperwork." Alexander's jaw tightened and he stared straight ahead, his knuckles white on the wheel as he drove. Realization came like a burst of lightning. "You told him to do it, didn't you? You talked him into getting the life insurance policy."

Alexander shrugged. "I suggested it. I simply had to mention that once an addict always an addict. Pressed home the point that he couldn't know for sure that you wouldn't revert to your old ways, that you might over-dose one day. It took some convincing, but he went along with it eventually. Just like everything I suggested." He cut his eyes to her. "Except when I told him not to marry you. His one defiance."

"He loved you. Practically worshipped you," Zoe said. Sickness curled in her belly. How did she not know about the policy? "When does the two-year contestability period end?"

"You know about that, huh?"

"Yes. When?"

"Today."

"That was you on the phone at the ranch," she whispered. "You called from Nina and Gregory's house when the men had Sophia and me at the Updike ranch. Didn't you? To tell them not to kill me because if they had—"

"Yes." He turned left and she frowned.

"Because if I died before today," she continued, "the insurance company has the right to take their time and investigate everything, delaying payment, but once the two-year con-testability period is passed, they'll pay out within thirty days." She closed her eyes and leaned her head against the window. "You've been planning to kill me for two years." It wasn't a question.

"It's nothing personal. I've made some bad investments. Even got Gregory and Nina involved. Gregory was smart, but I was too stubborn to listen to him when he told me to sell. I kept thinking the stock would turn around."

"But it didn't."

"No, it didn't. I've been managing to keep my head above water, but just barely. And now it's all about to come crashing down around me. Unless I come up with some big money in the next couple of months, I'm ruined." He shot her another sideways glance.

She felt light-headed. He talked about killing her like it was just another item to check off his daily to-do list. "Where does Brian fit in all of this?"

He glanced at her. "What do you mean?"

"He was the one who tried to break in last night. Aaron chased him, tackled him and pulled his mask off. He was in Nina and Gregory's house earlier and recognized him in a photo."

Alexander's nostrils flared and his jaw tightened. "I didn't realize he'd messed up so bad." The man heaved a sigh. "Well, at least I don't have to worry about him talking. There's no way anyone can connect him to me."

She stared at Alexander, the sick feeling building at the base of her throat. "What do you mean?"

He slid her a glance. "Shut up."

Grief pierced her and she knew that Brian was dead. "You killed him."

"I said shut up!"

"Why him?" she insisted. "Why involve him?" In spite of the trouble the man had brought down on her, she didn't wish him dead.

His fingers flexed on the wheel. "He wanted that stupid horse. I told him you'd stolen Sophia away from me and I just wanted to talk to you but I couldn't even get close to you. I told him if he would simply bring you to me using whatever means necessary, I'd sign the horse over to him."

"But you don't have the right to do that. The papers are in my name."

"Brian didn't know that."

She ran her palms down her thighs as her brain whirled. The man was sick. "You planned to kill him all along."

He shrugged. "Once you turned up dead, I couldn't have Brian going to the police, could I?"

"Of course not."

He frowned at her sarcasm. She bit her

tongue against the rest of the words she wanted to hurl at him, exercising extreme self-control to keep them from slipping from her lips. *Oh, God, please help me.*

"What were you doing at Nina and Gregory's the day the men attacked us?" she asked. "Are they in on this, too?"

"Of course not. Nina's pushy and likes things her way, but she doesn't have the stomach for something like this. And Gregory—" he snorted "—he's just a 'yes, ma'am' man when it comes to Nina. Whatever Nina says goes." He tapped the wheel and glanced in the rearview mirror. "I'd forgotten they were out of town when I stopped by. Gregory's been selling some of my wife's antique pieces and I needed to get a check from him. While I was there Pete called me on my burner phone, but the battery was almost dead. I was getting ready to get in the car and leave, but could tell the situation demanded immediate attention when I heard the gunshots. I went in the house to use the landline to call him back." His jaw flexed. "What are the odds that Pete's cell phone would fall into law enforcement hands and they'd trace the number back?"

"But they did. And they know someone was in touch with Pete the day everything happened at the ranch. Why do you think you can kill me now and—"

"Because I can," he snapped. "I have to." He shook his head. "Like I said, it's nothing personal. The money from your insurance policy goes to Sophia."

"And Sophia goes to Nina and Gregory as will the trust fund money," she said. "What are you going to do? Kill them, too?"

He snorted. "Nope. You're going to sign a codicil naming me as the beneficiary. I'll wait a month or so and miraculously find the paper and the money will be turned over to me. It's as simple as that. With you dead and Sophia in my custody, I'll have immediate access to her trust fund. And then your life insurance money will come in over the next few weeks and everything will fall into place."

"What about Sophia? What's going to happen to her?"

"Assuming you cooperate, Nina will get to keep Sophia. Nina was heartbroken you two refused to move in with her after Trevor died. She'll have no problem taking in her poor orphaned niece."

Cooperate. As in let him kill her. As in asking her to give her life so her child could live. She would. If she had to. But what would Sophia's life be like without Zoe? Raised by

Nina and Gregory? "Wait a minute, if you didn't want me dead before today, why try to kill me all those times?"

"I wasn't trying to kill you, I was trying to get rid of all of the watchdogs. They were guarding you so tight I couldn't get to you. Those idiots at the ranch nearly ruined everything. I hired them to kidnap the two of you, not start this incredible mess." She blinked and thought back to all of the times they'd been chased or shot at. Every time she'd had someone with her. She shuddered.

When he pulled into the drive of the Updike ranch, she gasped. "I want to see Sophia. Why are we coming here?"

"Because this is where you're going to realize the futility of your situation and resort to your old drug habits. Unfortunately, you overdose."

Horrified, she stared at the syringe he'd produced from seemingly out of nowhere. "I won't," she whispered.

"You will," he growled, "or Sophia dies. Your choice."

SIXTEEN

Aaron drummed his fingers on the door handle of the car as Clay drove and Lance gave him directions according to the GPS tracker. "Take a right here."

From the backseat, Aaron didn't have a good view of the electronic map system, but the route was familiar. He sat forward. "Wait a minute. That's taking us to the Updike farm. He's taking her out there. Why?"

"It's remote, no one's there," Lance said quietly.

Aaron sat back with a thump. "He's taking her there to kill her. Hurry up."

"Going as fast as I can," Clay said. "You know we're making a mighty big assumption that she's in that car."

"Mrs. Mayfield said she got in a white Cadillac," Aaron said. "The license plate matches the one we're following. I think it's a safe assumption she's in the car. I don't know who has her—Jed or Brian or even Collier himself, but Zoe's in that car and I'm guessing she was forced to make the decision to either get in or risk something happening to Sophia. We need to get to her as fast as possible."

Clay glanced at Lance. "I agree. Call for backup. Every unit available needs to head to the Updike farm."

The tension in Aaron's belly curled tighter. "We're still fifteen minutes away. A lot can happen in fifteen minutes."

Clay barked orders into the radio while Aaron sent up prayers for Zoe and Sophia's safety. How had this happened? How had Alexander gotten her out of the house right under their very noses? Where was Sophia? Was she with Alexander and Zoe?

Traffic on the road to the farm was heavy enough to slow them down slightly in spite of the fact that Clay had the siren going. They still had to slow down as people pulled over and maneuver safely through intersections. "Come on, Clay."

"Going as fast as I can."

Aaron prayed it was fast enough.

Zoe's panic tripled when Alexander stopped the car. He got out and shut the door then started around toward her side. She leaned over and with her bound hands pulled the cuff of her jeans up enough to get to the strap holding the small pistol in the ankle holster. She slipped it off and glanced up to see him almost at her door.

She pulled her pant leg down just as he opened the door and grasped her upper arm. He hauled her out. "Alexander, please don't do this."

"It's not like I really want to, Zoe. It's just the way things have worked out."

"Where's Ginny? How did you convince her to go along with you?"

"How do you know I did?"

"Because Ginny said something about massive amounts of security on Sophia's school and the house when I was determined to keep Sophia home today. Ginny convinced me Sophia would be safe because of it and it was the only reason I let her go. But there was no extra security. She had to think on her feet and make that up so she could get Sophia away from me."

"You always were a smart girl."

"Well?"

"Ginny has a special-needs sister in Nashville who loves her very expensive private group home. Unfortunately Ginny's parents have fallen on hard times. I simply offered to pay the girl's fees for the next year if she would let me protect Sophia. It took some convincing, but once the money was in her account she agreed. As long as I promised not to hurt Sophia." He rolled his eyes and placed a hand over his heart and mocked, "She's my granddaughter, my dead son's child, I would never hurt her. I just want the best for her. Look at all the danger she's in. Zoe may be willing to trust her life into the hands of the local sheriff's office, and that's her decision, but I want my granddaughter to have more protection than that. Please, Ginny, I can't do this without your help. Zoe won't let me get near her. I have money, I can hire bodyguards, but I can't do all that if she's not with me. What will it take to convince you?" Zoe couldn't take her eyes from him. He deserved an Oscar. His sincerity, his pleading eyes nearly convinced even her.

She could see how Ginny fell for it. Was that why Ginny had questioned Zoe the night Brian had tried to break into the house? Had she been feeling Zoe out? Trying to determine how Zoe felt about her father-in-law? Zoe felt sick. Never in a million years would she have suspected him capable of this kind of thing. He pushed her toward the barn and she stumbled along the snow-covered grass. "Why did you try to kidnap Sophia when she was on her way home from school? What purpose would that serve?"

"I was going to be the hero. I was going to pay the ransom, return your daughter to you and then talk you into making me guardian should anything happen to you. After all, it's obvious how much I loved and wanted her."

Zoe wanted to weep. "I never would have agreed."

"Sure you would have. You would have owed me. It's just the way you're wired. Then once the papers were signed and all legal, you would have suffered a terrible car accident at some point in the near future."

"Sometime after today," she said. Her voice sounded dull. Resigned. She had to get away from him. Sophia was safe for now. She'd thought he was taking her to Knoxville, that she would have more time to think, to plan her escape. But if she didn't do something fast, she was dead.

"Definitely after today."

Zoe stopped walking. "But you tried to run me off the road shortly after Sophia's kidnapping attempt. You could have killed me."

"Could have, but I didn't think it would. The point was to scare you into running to me for help." He gave her a rough shove that almost sent her to her knees.

She kept her balance. "But of course I didn't."

"No, of course not. That little plan backfired and sent you running, period."

"And yet you still managed to find me?"

He laughed. "I knew where you were two days after you left. You forget that I have friends in high places. Police officer friends who were very sympathetic to the fact that my daughter-in-law had taken my granddaughter and moved away without leaving her contact information. One had no trouble finding you and passing that information along to me."

Zoe's sinking feeling dipped lower. "Well, if you knew where I was the whole time, why wait a month to come after me?"

"It's all about the timing, Zoe. It takes time to plan these things. To research the people you associated with, to find the right people to hire to…find you."

"Time to plot my murder?"

"If you want to be crass about it." He stopped in front of the barn and held the gun steady on her. "But of course all that went down the drain because people are incompetent. I find that if I want things done right,

I just have to do them myself." He gestured toward the door. "Now get inside. You'll be safe in the barn."

"Safe?"

"Wrong word." He narrowed his eyes. "Hidden if you prefer. Regardless of what you call it, this will be a good place for you to pass out from your overdose. One of the hands will find you day after tomorrow."

He twisted to open the barn door and for just a moment he was distracted. She lifted a foot and planted it against the back of his right knee in a swift hard kick. He hollered and went down.

Zoe spun and took off around the side of the barn.

Clay rolled onto the Updike property at a slow crawl. "What are you doing?"

"Don't want to tip him off that we're here," Clay said. "We need to use caution. The GPS say he's still on the property?" he asked Lance.

"Yes, the car is here."

Aaron wanted to bolt from the backseat and go find Zoe, but he curbed his impatience. He sure didn't want to make a bad situation worse by being impulsive. "So what are we waiting for?"

"Backup," Clay said.

"Zoe might not have time for backup," Aaron hissed. "We need to find her now." He looked at the snow-covered ground. "Those tire tracks are fresh. All we have to do is follow them."

"We can't go busting in trying to find her. We could set him off if he realizes we know he's here."

"Then let's do a subtle search. I don't care how we do it, we just need to do it now." Clay hesitated then glanced at Lance. "What would you do if it was Sabrina?" Aaron pressed.

"Fine," Clay conceded. "But you stay back. You're not a cop."

"I'll stay back, just start looking."

Clay started following the tire tracks. Lance kept glancing first one way then the other. Aaron knew he was looking for a sniper. He had to admit that spot between his shoulder blades itched, but he hoped if the man who had Zoe was working alone, he was occupied with her, not parked on a hill waiting for someone to show up.

The tracks led to the barn.

He took one step and heard a muffled cry.

Zoe let out another scream as Alexander hauled her to her feet. He'd tackled her before she'd gotten too far. Desperation clawed at her. She kicked out and caught him in the chin. His fist cracked against her cheek. She dropped to the ground. Pain rocketed through her and for a moment the world spun. He dropped beside her and his hand gripped her upper arm.

"Zoe!"

She froze. Alexander froze. Then cursed. He planted the weapon against her head. "Make one more sound and I'll kill you right here."

She trembled, but stayed quiet. Then she heard them. Voices moving toward the barn. Alexander's harsh breathing echoed in her ear. She had to get away from him. But how? Still on the hard, cold ground, she could feel him waiting, his tension level near the snapping point. She pulled her leg up toward her hands.

Thankfully, he didn't seem to notice her movement as he kept his attention focused on the voices. Slowly, so slowly, she pulled the leg of her jeans up revealing the weapon still strapped to her ankle.

The sound of feet moving closer had Alexander's muscles bunching tighter. As well as his grip on her bicep. Just an inch farther, and she could wrap her fingers around the butt of

the gun. She shifted. "Be still," he snapped.
She stilled. If he looked down her body, he'd
see the gun in plain sight. But he didn't. As
soon as she obeyed, he turned back to the approaching men. He moved the barrel of the
weapon from the side of her head and aimed
it at Aaron. Her breath caught.

"Tracks end here," she heard Clay say softly.
"There's the white Cadillac."

Aaron spun, his eyes probing. Lance did
the same.

And Alexander adjusted his aim.

"Watch out!"

At Zoe's cry the three men ducked behind
the Cadillac, and Alexander gave a roar of
fury even as he brought the weapon around
to slam it against the side of her head. But she
was already moving, bending at the waist to
get the gun from the holster, and he caught
her with only a glancing blow to her shoulder.

She had her bound hands wrapped around
the gun. She pulled it from the holster as
Alexander turned his weapon back toward the
men. The crack of his gun made her ears ring,
but she didn't stop. She rolled and placed her
muzzle against Alexander's thigh and pulled
the trigger.

He cried out and dropped his weapon. Zoe
rolled to her knees and pushed herself to her

feet even while Alexander was scrambling for the gun. She stepped forward and planted her weapon against his temple. "Move and it will be the last thing you do."

"Zoe!" Clay hollered.

"Over here! Behind the barn!" The shakes wanted to set in, but she held strong. Aaron would be here in just a moment then she would be able to break down. Alexander glared up at her even while he clamped his hands around his wounded leg. Without a word to her, he reached into the pocket of his coat and pulled out the roll of duct tape.

"What are you doing?" she asked, breathless and trembling. "It's over," she said.

Instead of answering her, he pulled a long strip off the roll and started wrapping it around his leg and she realized he was making a tourniquet. Zoe backed up, the weapon still on him. With a grunt he ripped the rest of the strip and dropped the tape to the ground. He sat there, shoulders heaving, his features pale.

She continued her backward journey never taking her eyes from Alexander.

Clay and Lance rounded the corner of the barn, weapons raised. "Police! Freeze! Show your hands now!" Clay's harsh orders went ignored. Alexander didn't move.

A loud crack broke the air and dirt and snow spewed up from the ground beside Alexander. Zoe saw the flash come from the trees bordering the property. Who was there? Another officer?

She had no more time to wonder as Clay and Lance ducked back around the corner and Alexander surged to his feet and came after her. Zoe let out another cry and pulled the trigger. The bullet caught the man in the upper shoulder and he spun but didn't go down. He lunged around on his good leg and limped after her.

Zoe back-pedaled and turned to run, but her right foot came down on a large rock. Her ankle twisted and with a cry she tumbled to the ground unable to break her fall with her hands still taped together. Her weapon flew from her fingers, the air whooshed from her lungs.

In the distance a gunshot sounded and she jerked. Expected to feel a burst of pain, but nothing. Then a body slammed into her and she went to the ground one more time.

She felt a prick against her neck. "Now, if you move again," Alexander panted, "this heroin will make you one dead junkie, are we clear?"

She felt the warmth of the blood from his

shoulder wound against her back. She almost nodded and thought better of it. "Yes," she whispered.

Aaron, Lance and Clay appeared once again. Lance and Clay held their weapons ready as they took in the scene. She saw Aaron's hope slide from his face and horror take up residence.

"Get up," Alexander demanded. Zoe climbed painfully to her feet as did her very pale-faced father-in-law. "Tell them to back off now."

"Don't come over here, Aaron! He's got a syringe full of heroin he's threatening to inject me with. Back up, please."

Aaron blanched then stayed still. Lance and Clay stopped, but held their guns aimed in Alexander's direction.

"Good," Alexander whispered. "Now all I want is to get out of here. I'm going to use you to do that, understand?"

"Yes."

"We're going to walk around the barn and toward the car."

She started in the direction he ordered, and he limped along beside her, his breathing heavy against her ear. Once they rounded the side of the barn, she stopped and he stumbled against her. The needle pierced her neck, and she winced and pulled away. His grip on her arm tightened. She stared at the line of police cars and law enforcement officers parked in the yard. Aaron, Clay and Lance came into her line of sight from the other side of the barn. They were able to slip behind the cruiser to use it as protection in case other shots sounded. Zoe couldn't help but wonder who else was out there in the woods shooting. A sniper with the police department? Had the person meant to hit Alexander? Or had he been aiming for Zoe and just missed?

"Alexander, you're trapped," Clay called. "Let's end this now before anyone else gets hurt."

"The house," Alexander told her. "Go to the house."

Zoe didn't like the fact that he was completely ignoring Clay. He really thought he was going to find a way out of this. "Who shot you, Alexander?" she asked, her voice shaky and weak.

"A sniper, probably. A lousy shot if you ask me. Call your sniper off, Sheriff, or I'll make this a murder-suicide. You want that on your conscience?"

"It wasn't a sniper, Collier," Clay called. "We didn't have anyone up in the trees."

"Like I'm supposed to believe that?"

"It's true. If it were one of mine, you'd be on the ground dead, a bullet in your brain, not your shoulder."

Zoe cleared her throat and caught Aaron's eye and saw the intense worry in the lines of his face. Clay stood next to him as well as Lance. All three of them, as well as the other law enforcement officers, watched them. Zoe knew Alexander was either going to try and use her as a hostage to negotiate his way out. Failing that, she felt certain there would be a murder-suicide. With a sick certainty, she knew that if it came down to getting caught and going to prison or dying, he'd choose to die.

She was going to have to do something.

"You messed up, Zoe. Bad. Now Sophia is going to die," he told her.

She kept walking, her brain groping for any kind of way to get away from him. She knew he had enough of the drug in the syringe to kill her quickly. It would have an almost immediate effect. She'd feel sleepy, pass out and forget to breathe. And unless there was immediate medical attention, she'd die. But once she was in the house, she had almost no hope of surviving.

"Please, Alexander," she whispered. Begging him was futile, but she could hope for a distraction.

"Shut. Up." He leaned heavily against her. He turned her to face the deputies as he passed, shifting so he never had his back to them. Aaron took a step toward them. Clay pulled him back. Alexander stumbled. The needle went into the back of her neck. She cried out and tried to pull away from him.

"Zoe!" Aaron's cry spurred her. She spun into Alexander's grip, felt the syringe fall from her. Two shots rang out. Alexander fell at her feet.

She felt the effects of the drug and realized Alexander must have pressed the syringe. Dizziness hit her, she relaxed and fell to the ground and let the sensations sweep her even as darkness claimed her.

SEVENTEEN

Aaron paced outside Zoe's hospital room, his prayers for her never ceasing. Clay and Lance were also there working on paperwork even as they waited for Zoe to wake up. Clay stood at the nurse's station pounding on his laptop. Lance walked up and clapped Aaron on the shoulder. "She's going to be all right. She just fainted. The doc said there was very little trace of the drug in her system. Only slightly more than what was on the needle when Alexander pulled the liquid into the syringe."

"But there was some. He did manage to press the syringe before we stopped him."

"Yes, but not much."

"It might not matter," Aaron said. "It could still send her back into her addiction."

"I know," Lance said softly. "But she didn't pass out because of the drug. The doctor said she passed out due to the stress of the situation, and she really only needs to sleep and heal. We'll be thankful she didn't suffer any worse than some cuts and bruises."

"True."

"And we'll just pray that she doesn't even notice the small amount of the drug." He cleared his throat. "The good thing is Nina and Gregory didn't have any idea of what Collier was doing. They've got their lake house on the market to sell and are determined to help Zoe in any way they can."

"Zoe will be glad. She and her in-laws weren't super close, but she'll be relieved to know they didn't want her dead."

"Sophia is with them. I talked to her a little bit and told her that her mother wanted to see her real soon. She sounded happy. I let Nina tell her about Zoe being in the hospital."

"Can you send someone to pick Sophia up? She'll be the first face Zoe wants to see when wakes up."

"I'm way ahead of you. Nina's driving her here herself."

Aaron nodded. "Great. Did you find the jockey?"

"Yes. He had a single gunshot wound to the back of his head. A hiker found him just outside of Knoxville in a wooded area. It's amazing he was found this fast. He was really off the beaten path."

Sadness filled Aaron. The man had brought about his death with his own greed, but Aaron thought the punishment didn't fit the crime. Cartee had wanted the horse, and Alexander had used that desire to fuel his greed. Definitely sad. "What about the shot that came from the trees and hit Alexander in the shoulder? That wasn't one of your guys?"

"Nope. Parker made his way up there after the shot and found the shooter. It was Jedediah Mason. Parker shot him before Jed could get off another shot. He's dead."

Aaron closed his eyes for a brief moment. So much death. And it was so senseless and unneeded. "What was he doing up there?"

"Trying to shoot Alexander apparently. Before he died he said something about no honor among thieves. Alexander had backed out on paying him."

"So he was going to kill Alexander."

"Yep."

"How's Ginny?"

"Hanging in there. She woke up and was able to tell Clay what happened."

Ginny had been found not too far from her wrecked vehicle with a bullet in her side. "She pretty much verified the evidence they gathered at the scene. And the school phone records traced back to her cell. She was the one who called the school and pretended to be Zoe."

Aaron winced. "Okay. Then what?"

"She'd arranged to meet Alexander and give him Sophia. He'd deposited ten grand in her account to pay for her sister to be able to stay in her home."

Aaron sucked in a breath. "Collier did his homework, didn't he?"

"He did. After he learned where Zoe was, he started investigating into the pasts of all of us on the police force to figure out which person might possibly be open to his schemes."

"And he discovered Ginny's weakness."

"Yep. She said he called her and told her he knew Zoe was in trouble and was worried about Sophia being caught in the middle. He asked her to help him at least get Sophia away from everything. When she hesitated, he told her he knew about her sister and was willing to help her if she would help him."

"So she met Collier and gave him Sophia. Why shoot her? The money was already in her account. It's not like he could get it back."

Lance shrugged. "I figured it was because he didn't want any witnesses. But she said she changed her mind and refused to hand Sophia over to him."

Aaron blinked. "You believe her?"

Lance nodded. "Yes, I do. She was weeping and begging my forgiveness."

"So he shot her."

"Shot her and left her for dead. He destroyed the cruiser's radio and took her cell phone. She said Brian Cartee was there, too."

Aaron sighed and pinched the bridge of his nose. "Man."

"Yeah. Ginny said she played dead until Alexander, Brian and Sophia drove off. She hated to just let them take Sophia, but figured if they knew she was alive, she wouldn't have the chance to let anyone know who Sophia was with. When they were gone, she managed to walk until she passed out. She rolled down into the ditch—the reason it took so long to find her."

A nurse stepped out of the room and smiled at Aaron. "Mrs. Collier is awake and asking for two people. Aaron and Sophia?"

"I'm Aaron. Sophia's on her way. May I see Zoe?"

"Of course."

She stepped aside, and Aaron slipped through the open door. The room was dark so he opened the blinds then turned toward the woman who'd come to mean more to him than breathing itself. "Hey." He stepped up to the bed and took her hand.

"Hey," she said. "Where's Sophia? Is she all right?"

Her fear nearly undid him. "She's fine. Nina's on the way right now bringing her to you."

Tears filled her eyes and dripped down her temples. Aaron grabbed a handful of tissues from the box on her end table and dried the wetness. "No need to cry. Really, she's just fine."

"Oh, thank you, God."

"Yes."

She sniffed. "I've been so angry with Him."

"Who?"

"God. First my baby was diagnosed with diabetes, then Trevor was killed and I felt so guilty."

He sat down beside her. "Why? Why guilty?"

"Because he didn't deserve me. He deserved someone so much better." She sighed and closed her eyes. "I loved him, but I loved him because he was…safe. Solid and secure. I've always felt guilty that I didn't love him… more. And then he was killed and I never had the chance."

"He was what you needed at the time."

"Oh, yes, he was definitely that."

"Was he happy?"

She smiled, a sad little curve of her lips.

"Yes. I can honestly say he was happy. We had a good life and he loved Sophia with his whole heart."

He gripped her fingers. "I don't think you give yourself enough credit. You're amazing."

She gave a half laugh, half sob. "Amazing? No, not really."

He leaned over and kissed her. When he pulled back she was staring at him. "Do you trust me?" he asked.

"Yes."

He smiled. "I like that there wasn't any hesitation there."

"How could I not trust you? You've put your own life ahead of mine."

"Just like you did with Sophia."

"Of course."

"So if you would do that for your child, then don't you think God would do that for you?"

She paused. Then nodded. "Yes, he would. He did. He sent his only son to die for me."

"Exactly. So don't bash yourself. You are made in His image, and He felt you were worth dying for. That makes you amazing."

She looked down at her hands. "I never thought about it like that," she whispered. "I've never thought I was worth much of anything. My parents didn't think I was worth fighting for. My brother didn't think I was worth hanging around for, and I guess I've always wondered why Trevor loved me like he did."

"Was Trevor a Christian?"

"Yes." She smiled. "He was."

"Then he saw what I see, what God sees. A beautiful woman, inside and out. A mother who loves her child enough to die for her. A woman who puts others above herself. Don't you see that?"

Red flooded her face, and Aaron hugged her. "No, not really. But I guess when you put it that way…" she mumbled against his shoulder. She leaned back. "I just felt so…betrayed by God. I'd struggled to get clean, to get my life on track and I know He was there with me every step of the way. And then I got mad at Him when Sophia developed diabetes, three years ago. Then Trevor died, and it's just been a hard year." She gave a small shrug. "And then I met you and knowing what your family has been through up to this point and seeing their faithfulness has been a real eye-opener. I want that kind of faith, as well."

"You have it."

"Well, I'm definitely working on it."

"We'll work on it together if you'll let me." He paused and took a deep breath. "I love you, Zoe." She gasped and stared up at him. He shrugged. "Call me crazy, but I do. I've known you were the one for me from the time we met at the diner." He tapped her chin and her mouth shut with a snap. "I can see I've shocked you. You don't have to say anything, but I wanted to tell you what's in my heart. I don't want you to leave, but if you feel you have to move back to Knoxville, I'll follow you. I can set up a practice anywhere, but I just don't want to lose you. Unless you want me to get lost." Uncertainty filled him, her stunned expression keeping him from being able to breathe.

She studied him then shook her head. "I don't know what to say."

"Do you want me to get lost?"

"No! No, not at all."

"Well, that's a relief." He smiled and she gave a low laugh. He turned serious again. "If you don't want me to get lost, just tell me what's in your heart."

She drew in a deep breath and let it out slowly then nodded. "I have to say, my heart's pretty full right now."

"Good to hear."

She plucked at the sheet with her free hand then looked him in the eye. "I had a good life back in Knoxville, some good friends I look forward to reconnecting with now that I wouldn't be putting any of them in danger. But I think I've come to realize that my life there is now a part of my past. When we arrived in Wrangler's Corner, it was a bit like coming home. And even during all the craziness, every time I thought about leaving, I would get this hollow ache in my stomach."

"So what are you saying?"

"I'm saying I want to stay here. Sophia loves it. She loves you."

He understood how she felt when she said her heart was full. Something else they had in common. "And what about her mother?"

Zoe swallowed and pulled in a deep breath. Butterflies settled in her stomach and she wondered if she could even get the words she wanted to say through the tightness in her throat. "Her mother loves you, too, Aaron." His hands tightened around hers. "I think I've loved you from the moment you carried Sophia across that river, protecting her as though she were your own."

"I want her to be."

And then she couldn't speak anymore. He leaned over and kissed her as though the only way he could tell her he loved her was through the kiss. She wrapped her arms around his neck and pulled him closer.

"Does this mean you're getting married?"

Zoe yanked back with a gasp. "Sophia!" She held her arms open and Sophia ran across the small space to hop on the bed and snuggled down next to her. "I've missed you!"

"I missed you, too, but I had fun with Aunt Nina." She frowned and gently touched the bruises Alexander had left on Zoe's face. "Are you okay? I was scared when Aunt Nina said we had to come to the hospital to see you. Did the bad men come back and hurt you?"

Zoe's eyes met Nina's red-rimmed and puffy ones. "I'm fine, honey. Just a little accident, that's all. All the bad men are gone, and we're safe as we can be. My wounds will heal." *Thank you, God.*

A brilliant smile broke out on Sophia's face, and her eyes looked lighter than they had in weeks. Zoe's heart ached at the stress the past few weeks had brought into her child's life. But that was over now. Sophia hugged her again. "I'm glad. Is Ginny okay, too? Her car broke down, and Grandpop came along to help. Isn't that crazy?"

"Hmm. Yes. Crazy." How much had Sophia seen with the incident that had landed Ginny in the hospital with a gunshot wound?

Aaron came to kneel in front of Sophia. He took her hand in his. "What exactly happened with Ginny's car breaking down?"

Sophia shrugged. "I'm not really sure. Ginny said her car broke down so she called someone to come help us. Brian and Grandpop showed up. Grandpop asked Ginny if he could help her and she said no, that was all right, she was waiting for someone else."

"She did?" Zoe asked.

"Yes. She said something about changing her mind, and Grandpop got really mad. He told Brian to take me to the car while he and Ginny talked. So I went with Brian, but the car was pretty far away and I couldn't tell if Grandpop got her car started again or not."

"What happened to Brian after you got in the car with Grandpop?" Just saying the man's name made her want to gag. She looked up to see tears streaming down Nina's face. Aaron passed the box of tissues over to Nina and she grabbed several.

"I don't know," Sophia said. "Grandpop drove me to Nina's, and then he and Brian went somewhere."

She shuddered as she thought of the end Brian had met. So Alexander had dropped Sophia off then killed Brian. At least Sophia had been spared seeing Ginny hurt. Which led her to believe Alexander had been serious about leaving Sophia with Nina and Gregory. He hadn't wanted her traumatized—or a witness—to his violence. Zoe sent up a prayer of thankfulness that her child had been spared that.

Aaron hugged Sophia. "I'm glad you're all right, kid."

Sophia leaned back, grasped his face between her hands and kissed his nose. "Thanks, Doctor Aaron. I'm fine." She glanced at her mother then back to Aaron. "So are you going to marry my mom?"

Aaron flushed, but Zoe loved that he didn't look away from Sophia. "If she'll have me."

"Oh, *we* will," Sophia said.

Zoe gave a choked laugh. "And that's that, huh?"

Sophia grinned at her. "Of course."

Nina sniffed and blew out a sigh. Her gaze danced between Zoe and Aaron. "It looks like you have some unfinished business here. Is it all right if Sophia stays with me at the hotel tonight?" At Zoe's hesitation, Nina lifted a hand. "It's fine, I understand why you might not want to."

Zoe glanced at Aaron then Sophia. "I just hate for you to have to stay at a hotel. You're welcome to stay at the house and use my room." Sophia's shoulders slumped and Zoe raised a brow. "But maybe if Sophia wants to stay at the hotel, it could be arranged." She ran a hand over her child's soft hair. "What do you want to do?"

Sophia slanted her eyes at her aunt. "They have an indoor pool, right?"

Nina laughed and swiped her nose with the tissue. "Yes, they do."

Sophia nodded and turned to Zoe. "I think I'd like to go with Aunt Nina if that's all right."

"But you don't have a swimsuit."

Sophia's cheeks turned red, and she dropped her gaze. She shuffled her feet then looked up at Zoe through her lashes. "Well, I *might* have overheard Aunt Nina and Uncle Gregory making plans about bringing me to see you and she *might* have mentioned staying at the Marriott just outside of Wrangler's Corner and everybody knows they have an indoor pool…" She lifted her hands—the picture of innocence.

"So you *might* have packed the bathing suit you usually keep at Nina's?"

"I *might* have."

"All right, you can go."

Sophia squealed and gave Zoe another hug, turned to Aaron and held up her arms. He picked her up, and she squeezed his neck. Then she scurried down and raced to her aunt's side to grasp the woman's hand.

They turned to go and Nina looked back over her shoulder. "Thank you," she whispered.

Zoe nodded. "Thank you. For everything."

When the door shut behind them Aaron moved back to his spot on the bed. "Now. Where were we?"

She felt the heat rise in her cheeks. "Um—"

"Oh, yes, I remember." He lowered his head once more and captured her lips for yet another tender kiss. When he pulled back, he studied her. She shifted and gave a small laugh. "What?"

"You don't seem to have any lingering side effects from the drug."

She let her smile fall away. "No. Not right now." She bit her lip. "Aaron, I want…" She stopped and twisted the sheet into a ball then smoothed it back over her legs.

He covered her fidgeting hands with his. "What? What do you want, Zoe?"

She met his gaze. "I want to explore what we have. I want it more than anything, but you have to understand what you're getting into if you decide you want to be with me.

I've been clean for over ten years—discounting today."

"I don't count today."

His tenderness made her want to cry, but she had to make sure he understood. "There are still days I struggle, Aaron. Not as many after all this time, true, but there *are* days I want a hit."

"But you don't get one."

"No. I don't, but it can be very difficult for me—and those around me—until it passes."

He cupped her cheek. "I can handle it. What do you do when the craving hits?"

"I either eat chocolate or go running. Or both."

"Excellent."

She lifted a brow. "Why?"

"Those are two things I can do with you."

"Really?" A tear slipped out. She couldn't help it.

He swiped it away. "Really."

"If you're sure. Please be very, very sure."

He kissed her again then leaned his forehead against hers. "Look at me." She did. "I love you. Not one of us is perfect or without baggage, but together we can overcome that and build a great life together. Us and Sophia. The Three Musketeers, okay?"

She gave a relieved, watery laugh. "Okay, that sounds like a deal."

He kissed her again. "Definitely a deal."

She pulled back again. "I have a question."

"What's that?"

"Did Clay and Sabrina ever name their baby?"

Aaron blinked then a laugh burst from him. "Yes. They named her Hannah."

"Oh, that's a lovely name."

"We think so."

"Okay, that's all I wanted to know. You can kiss me again."

So he did.

EPILOGUE

Thanksgiving

Zoe stared at the huge family around the monster table. Mrs. Starke was in her element, and she beamed as she presided over the organized chaos. There were people everywhere, spilling in and out of every room, upstairs and down. Zoe had given up trying to remember names. Sophia played with two other little girls about her age and was giddy with excitement. She'd never had a holiday such as the one playing out now.

And neither had Zoe. Arms slipped around her waist from behind, and Zoe tilted her head to smile up at her fiancé. "Are you overwhelmed?" he asked.

"Completely, but it's lovely. Fascinating. This is how you grew up?"

"Every year at every holiday. Of course it's a lot bigger now, but yes, it was just as nuts back when I was a kid, too." He chuckled. "Dad had to clean out the barn and set up tables in front of all the stalls. He's got the heaters running, and the kids will eat out there with a few adult chaperones."

"All your cousins are here. Aunts, uncles." A familiar face stepped into the foyer. "And Lance, too."

"Lance has become part of the family. He doesn't have a lot of his own so we've sort of adopted him."

"You're good people, you Starkes," she said.

"Thanks." He looked up and froze.

Zoe slipped out of his arms and followed his gaze. "What is it?" Before he could answer, she saw the reason for his stillness. "Amber!" She waded through the mass of humanity and reached her longtime friend. Amber grinned and held out her arms. Zoe grabbed her in a big hug. "I'm so glad you're here. I can't tell you how grateful I am you sent me out here."

She shot a subtle glance at her brother. "I'd say Aaron owes me."

Zoe giggled. "Big time."

Amber gave another laugh, this one a bit more subdued. "I have a question for you, Zoe."

Zoe stilled. "What's that?"

"Will you step outside with me for a minute?"

"What's going on?" Aaron asked. He slid an arm across Zoe's shoulder and she leaned into him.

But curiosity had her eyeing Amber. "Sure, I'll step outside with you."

"I'm coming, too," Aaron said.

Amber nodded and the three of them slipped out the front door onto the big wrap-around porch. People still mingled in the chilly afternoon air, but at least it was quieter than the house. "What is it?"

"If I told you that I found your brother, would you want to see him?"

The words hung in the air while Zoe fought for breath. "Yes," she was finally able to gasp. "Yes, I'd love to see him."

Amber seemed to lose some of her tension. "Good." She looked at the far end of the porch. "See that guy sitting down there?"

Zoe turned to look and caught her breath when her eyes landed on the man Amber indicated. She'd know him anywhere. He was older, but it was him. "Toby?" He stood and faced her. Her older brother, her friend, and at one point in her life, her protector. She walked up and stood in front of him. Tears threatened, but she held them back. "I've missed you."

Tears gathered in his own eyes and he stepped forward to wrap her in his arms and bury his nose in her hair. "Oh, man, Zoe, I've missed you, too."

"Where have you been?"

"It's a long story."

"I've got time if you do."

"All I can say is I didn't mean to desert you. Abandon you all those years ago. But Dad was so awful, he told me that you hated me and never wanted to see me again."

Zoe gaped. "That's not true!"

"I know that now thanks to Amber, but at the time, after that fight, I believed him. You were so mad at me for leaving and going to college."

"I tried to tell you I was sorry, that I didn't mean it, but I couldn't find you," she whispered.

He closed his eyes. "It's not your fault. I did a little disappearing act. I joined the Marines about a month after I left. And then from there, I went to work for the government."

"In what capacity?"

He hesitated. "I can't tell you."

She blinked. "You have one of those jobs."

He gave a self-conscious smile. "Yes. I shouldn't have even told you that much, but

I'm going to have to disappear again, and I don't want you feeling abandoned yet again."

"But I've just found you. I don't want you to leave." She sounded like a five-year-old and didn't care.

Toby hugged her then Amber. "I can stay for a day or so, then will have to take off." His lips turned down. "I'm sorry, it's all I've got."

Zoe nodded and swiped a few stray tears. "I'll take it."

"Great. Now you want to introduce me to the guy who's been watching you like a lovesick puppy?"

Zoe and Amber laughed and Aaron grinned. She made the introductions and then jumped when a bell sounded. Aaron grabbed her hand. "Dinner is ready."

Zoe tucked her hand in his. "Let's go eat."

They found their way to one of the large tables and Aaron pulled her seat out for her. He introduced her to those around her. Seth, Aaron's brother, had a baby boy tucked into the crook of his left arm. "Seth's riding in the National Finals Rodeo the first week in December. Again."

"Congratulations, that's huge."

Seth grinned at her. "Thanks, and it's nice

to meet you. Didn't think anyone would lasso this brother of mine. You caught a good one."

Tonya, Seth's wife, smacked his arm—the one without the baby. "Really, Seth? Behave."

He ducked. "Sorry." Zoe didn't see any remorse in his bright blue eyes.

"Who's the little one?" she asked.

"That's Brady. He's three months old." Pride beamed from Seth's face. Sabrina came and swooped little Brady right out of his daddy's arm.

She grinned at Zoe. "Hi. My mom has Hannah so I'm going to just love on this little doll for a few minutes."

Zoe nodded. "I don't blame you a bit."

Aaron leaned over. "Do you think you can handle this crazy crew on a permanent basis?"

Butterflies swarmed in her stomach as his warm breath caressed her ear. She gripped his fingers. "I think I can handle anything with you at my side," she told him.

His eyes brightened and he bent down to steal a kiss in front of everyone. She knew her cheeks were as red as Sabrina's fire-engine top, but she didn't care a bit.

Sophia squealed and grabbed his arm to

hug it to her chest. "I'm glad you're marrying my mom."

"I am, too, sweetheart."

Sophia tilted her head and stared up at him. "So…"

"Yes?" Aaron asked.

"Can I call you 'Daddy'?" The question was so faint Zoe almost didn't hear it.

But the craziness around them faded as she watched Aaron pick Sophia up into his strong, capable arms. He kissed her cheek and settled her on his lap. "I can't think of anything that I would like more." He paused and slid an arm around Zoe's shoulders to pull her next to him. She could hardly breathe through the emotions filling her. Sophia smiled, a shy, gap-toothed smile. Then she looked at Aaron's mother, Mrs. Starke, who'd walked around the table to stand next to them. Tears glistened in her eyes.

"Doctor Aaron's going to be my daddy and you're going to be my grandma."

The woman nodded. "That's the best news I've heard today."

Sophia slid off her future daddy's lap and back into her chair. "I'm hungry."

Aaron still had his arm around Zoe's shoulder. He kissed her ear. "And I'm blessed."

"Correction. We're blessed."

"Amen to that." He kissed her again. "Now, the kid's hungry. Let's eat."

* * * * *

Dear Reader,

Thanks for coming along with me on Aaron and Zoe's journey. I love this next installment in the Wrangler's Corner series and hope you've enjoyed it, too! Zoe had quite the past to overcome: her parents' troubled marriage, her daughter's diabetes, her husband's death, her brother's disappearance… Wow! I really put her through it, didn't I? But she got through it. God was right by her side the entire way. Even though Zoe had given up on God, He hadn't given up on her. Amber sent her to the farm where Aaron and his family showed up and took her and Sophia under their wing to protect and shelter. I look at that and compare it to my own life. How God sends people at the right time and the right place for various reason—but all to help me. I hope you have someone in your life whom you know God has put there for a purpose. Just look around, I'm sure you'll figure it out!

God Bless,
Lynette

LARGER-PRINT BOOKS!

GET 2 FREE
LARGER-PRINT NOVELS
PLUS 2 FREE
MYSTERY GIFTS

Love Inspired®

Larger-print novels are now available...

YES! Please send me 2 FREE LARGER-PRINT Love Inspired® novels and my 2 FREE mystery gifts (gifts are worth about $10). After receiving them, if I don't wish to receive any more books, I can return the shipping statement marked "cancel." If I don't cancel, I will receive 6 brand-new novels every month and be billed just $5.49 per book in the U.S. or $5.99 per book in Canada. That's a savings of at least 19% off the cover price. It's quite a bargain! Shipping and handling is just 50¢ per book in the U.S. and 75¢ per book in Canada.* I understand that accepting the 2 free books and gifts places me under no obligation to buy anything. I can always return a shipment and cancel at any time. Even if I never buy another book, the two free books and gifts are mine to keep forever.

122/322 IDN GH6D

Name	(PLEASE PRINT)	
Address		Apt. #
City	State/Prov.	Zip/Postal Code

Signature (if under 18, a parent or guardian must sign)

Mail to the **Reader Service:**
IN U.S.A.: P.O. Box 1867, Buffalo, NY 14240-1867
IN CANADA: P.O. Box 609, Fort Erie, Ontario L2A 5X3

**Are you a current subscriber to Love Inspired® books
and want to receive the larger-print edition?
Call 1-800-873-8635 or visit www.ReaderService.com.**

* Terms and prices subject to change without notice. Prices do not include applicable taxes. Sales tax applicable in N.Y. Canadian residents will be charged applicable taxes. Offer not valid in Quebec. This offer is limited to one order per household. Not valid to current subscribers to Love Inspired Larger-Print books. All orders subject to credit approval. Credit or debit balances in a customer's account(s) may be offset by any other outstanding balance owed by or to the customer. Please allow 4 to 6 weeks for delivery. Offer available while quantities last.

Your Privacy—The Reader Service is committed to protecting your privacy. Our Privacy Policy is available online at www.ReaderService.com or upon request from the Reader Service.

We make a portion of our mailing list available to reputable third parties that offer products we believe may interest you. If you prefer that we not exchange your name with third parties, or if you wish to clarify or modify your communication preferences, please visit us at www.ReaderService.com/consumerschoice or write to us at Reader Service Preference Service, P.O. Box 9062, Buffalo, NY 14240-9062. Include your complete name and address.

LILP15

REQUEST YOUR FREE BOOKS!
2 FREE WHOLESOME ROMANCE NOVELS IN LARGER PRINT
PLUS 2 FREE MYSTERY GIFTS

⁂⁂⁂⁂⁂⁂⁂⁂⁂⁂⁂⁂⁂⁂⁂⁂⁂⁂⁂

HEARTWARMING™

⁂⁂⁂⁂⁂⁂⁂⁂⁂⁂⁂⁂⁂⁂⁂⁂⁂⁂⁂

Wholesome, tender romances

YES! Please send me 2 FREE Harlequin® Heartwarming Larger-Print novels and my 2 FREE mystery gifts (gifts worth about $10). After receiving them, if I don't wish to receive any more books, I can return the shipping statement marked "cancel." If I don't cancel, I will receive 4 brand-new larger-print novels every month and be billed just $5.24 per book in the U.S. or $5.99 per book in Canada. That's a savings of at least 19% off the cover price. It's quite a bargain! Shipping and handling is just 50¢ per book in the U.S. and 75¢ per book in Canada.* I understand that accepting the 2 free books and gifts places me under no obligation to buy anything. I can always return a shipment and cancel at any time. Even if I never buy another book, the two free books and gifts are mine to keep forever.

161/361 IDN GHX2

Name _____ (PLEASE PRINT)

Address _____ Apt. #

City _____ State/Prov. _____ Zip/Postal Code

Signature (if under 18, a parent or guardian must sign)

Mail to the **Reader Service:**
IN U.S.A.: P.O. Box 1867, Buffalo, NY 14240-1867
IN CANADA: P.O. Box 609, Fort Erie, Ontario L2A 5X3

* Terms and prices subject to change without notice. Prices do not include applicable taxes. Sales tax applicable in N.Y. Canadian residents will be charged applicable taxes. Offer not valid in Quebec. This offer is limited to one order per household. Not valid for current subscribers to Harlequin Heartwarming larger-print books. All orders subject to credit approval. Credit or debit balances in a customer's account(s) may be offset by any other outstanding balance owed by or to the customer. Please allow 4 to 6 weeks for delivery. Offer available while quantities last.

Your Privacy—The Reader Service is committed to protecting your privacy. Our Privacy Policy is available online at www.ReaderService.com or upon request from the Reader Service.

We make a portion of our mailing list available to reputable third parties that offer products we believe may interest you. If you prefer that we not exchange your name with third parties, or if you wish to clarify or modify your communication preferences, please visit us at www.ReaderService.com/consumerchoice or write to us at Reader Service Preference Service, P.O. Box 9062, Buffalo, NY 14240-9062. Include your complete name and address.

HW15

YES! Please send me **The Montana Mavericks Collection** in Larger Print. This collection begins with 3 FREE books and 2 FREE gifts (gifts valued at approx. $20.00 retail) in the first shipment, along with the other first 4 books from the collection! If I do not cancel, I will receive 8 monthly shipments until I have the entire 51-book Montana Mavericks collection. I will receive 2 or 3 FREE books in each shipment and I will pay just $4.99 US/ $5.89 CDN for each of the other four books in each shipment, plus $2.99 for shipping and handling per shipment.*If I decide to keep the entire collection, I'll have paid for only 32 books, because 19 books are FREE! I understand that accepting the 3 free books and gifts places me under no obligation to buy anything. I can always return a shipment and cancel at any time. My free books and gifts are mine to keep no matter what I decide.

263 HCN 2404 463 HCN 2404

Name	(PLEASE PRINT)
Address	Apt. #
City	State/Prov.	Zip/Postal Code

Signature (if under 18, a parent or guardian must sign)

Mail to the **Reader Service:**
IN U.S.A.: P.O. Box 1867, Buffalo, NY 14240-1867
IN CANADA: P.O. Box 609, Fort Erie, Ontario L2A 5X3

MMLPBPA15

READERSERVICE.COM

Manage your account online!

- Review your order history
- Manage your payments
- Update your address

> *We've designed the*
> *Reader Service website*
> *just for you.*

Enjoy all the features!

- Discover new series available to you, and read excerpts from any series.
- Respond to mailings and special monthly offers.
- Connect with favorite authors at the blog.
- Browse the Bonus Bucks catalog and online-only exculsives.
- Share your feedback.

Visit us at:

ReaderService.com

RS15